Baby You're a Star

The Rise and Rise of Pop Svengali, Louis Walsh

by Kathy Foley

Maverick House

Baby You're a Star

Copyright © Kathy Foley, 2002

The moral right of the author has been asserted

First published in Ireland in 2002
by Maverick House,
Unit 115, Ashbourne Industrial Estate,
Ashbourne, Co. Meath
email: info@maverickhouse.com

This edition 2002

ISBN 0-9542945-1-3

ACKNOWLEDGEMENTS

Top of the list are my publishers, Maverick House. Thanks so much for inviting me to write this book and for your support and advice throughout its production. Your faith and patience is much appreciated!

Thanks too to Louis Walsh who gave generously of his time and contacts, although he was under no obligation to do so. I'm also grateful to his family particularly Maureen, Frank and Evelyn Walsh, who agreed to be interviewed and supplied photos from their own collections.

Thanks must also go to all the other people who agreed to give interviews not forgetting everyone who helped to organise those interviews, gathered other information and offered photos, particularly Anto Byrne, Christina Thornbury, Jane Curtis, Lisa Brindley, Rosie Hunter, Joice Toh, Karola Zakrzewska, Alex, Caroline and Laura at Polydor, Nikki Shand at BMG, Michelle and Troy at Hot Press, Leanne at Aiken Promotions, Claire at the POD, James Sellar, Peter Robinson, Carol Hanna, Des Kiely, Anne Kearney and Declan Ryan in the Irish Examiner, Betty Solan of Kiltimagh Historical Society, the staff of IRD Kiltimagh and the staff of the National Library of Ireland.

Special thanks to all interviewees, especially Niall Stokes of Hot Press, Shay Healy, Tommy Hayden, Linda Martin, Barbara Mumba, John Coughlan, Mark Frith and Michael Ross.

Thanks also to Photocall Ireland and the Irish Examiner for supplying photographs.

I would also like to express my gratitude to the people who gave me a chance at different times in the past, and from whom I have learned the most along the way. Thanks to Eddie Holt, Peadar Kirby, Niall O'Dowd, Mark Keenan, Rob Norton, Neil McIntosh and everyone in Editorial and Production at Scope, including Charlie (for providing vital equipment!) and Dave (for not forgetting a poor freelancer!).

To Darina, thanks for making a kid welcome in the big city and teaching her a hell of a lot in the process. It meant more than you'll ever know and I promise I'll see those kids before they graduate!

Karen and Siobhan, we went through a lot of hassle in that bloody dump but I'd do it all again to make such great pals. The white waan and the stein of beer are on me, ladies.

Huge thanks too to all the girls from Cork – Cassandra, Eimear, Ciara, Maeve, Helena and Catherine (honourary Corkonian) – for putting up with my errant ways and far too occasional appearances. Special mention for Kate – we might not see each other as often as we should but the old friends are the best ones.

I can't forget the lads from Cork either (and yes, that includes you, Dom). Thanks for looking after himself when he was looking after me. I would mention you all by name but if I left anyone out, I would never be allowed to forget it, and if I listed all of you, there would be no room left for the rest of the book.

I must also thank those excellent friends who double up as professional advisers. Hanners, I'll visit you soon, I promise. Same goes for you, Ciara, if you ever up sticks to Rangendingendingdong. Joe Cam, please keep me in your portfolio – you'll always be in mine. Col, take a bow, you're my favourite charming man. Bourkie, thanks for all your help. By the way Ken, Lorcan, Tracy, Eiméar and Nora, look after these people. I need them!

Thanks too to the people who had the most to put up with. Rory, you're the barbecue king. Canice, the word count is . . . finished! Fiona, you're a rock. You kept me calm, fed and moisturised and a girl can't ask for more. Thanks to Glenn, Bronagh and Kevin as well and not forgetting Mr. and Mrs. Ferguson of Foxrock.

I've kept the best 'til last. Fred, you're the best brother in the wurrled! Some day I'll make it all up to you. Mum and Dad, thanks for supporting me and believing in me all the way. I would never have made it this far without you both.

And Giz, you know this book wouldn't exist without you. As always, thank you for making me laugh and keeping me sane. When my ship comes in, you'll be the first to board.

TABLE OF CONTENTS

POP SVENGALI

Pop: 'music of general appeal'
Svengali: 'one who exerts a malign persuasiveness
on another'

For any young wannabe pop star in Ireland, Louis Walsh is the way, the truth, and the light. He is Mr. Pop, the Pop King, the venerated god of Irish pop. He has guided his selected protégés to 22 No. 1 singles and six No. 1 albums in the UK, and many more No. 1s across Europe and Asia. He steered Samantha Mumba to No. 1 in the US, something few Irish or British pop managers have succeeded in doing. In short, he is Ireland's one and only pop svengali.

Svengali is a word often used to describe music managers at the pinnacle of their powers. Svengalis are the manager-gurus, the best of the best, those who are remembered along with the acts they managed. There was Brian Epstein and the Beatles, Peter Grant and Led Zeppelin, and Malcolm McLaren and the Sex Pistols. Modern-day svengalis include Paul McGuinness, the manager of U2; Simon Fuller, the manager of the Spice Girls; Lou Pearlman, the former manager of the Backstreet Boys and 'N Sync; and of course, Louis Walsh, the manager of almost every successful pop act to emerge from Ireland.

The original Svengali was a character in George du Maurier's successful novel *Trilby*, published in 1894. Svengali was a Hungarian hypnotist and singing master, who transformed a young French girl named Trilby into Europe's leading soprano, and lived in luxury on the proceeds of her concerts. The word "svengali" slipped into everyday use to mean a person who moulds others into musical sensations. The word in its original form was negative. Svengali's character was cruel and evil; he used his influence to mould his young protégée into a captivating singer, and exploited her for his own gain. Thus the dictionary definition of svengali as "one who exerts a malign persuasiveness on another".

With the passing of time, the word has altered in connotation and interpretation. Modern-day svengalis no longer exercise a malign influence on their protégés; they act as their guardians, guiding them through turbulence and difficulty. They still need to be persuasive and influential, however.

Pop svengalis like Louis Walsh are rare commodities. As with any profession, there are music managers who are mediocre, vast numbers who get the job done, and a select few who excel.

James Fisher, general secretary of the artist managers industry body, the Music Managers Forum (MMF), has a theory on this. To really succeed, he says, managers like Louis Walsh must be "single-minded and bloody-minded".

"Successful managers are fairly bloodsome [sic]," according to Fisher. "They're fairly difficult, because they've got to fight all the time. They've got to be very sure of their ground. You can't be woolly as an artist-manager. Even if you make the wrong decision, which you'll do, you've got to make decisions."

Band managers are not like managers in other industries. They don't sit in enormous leather swivel chairs smoking cigars and deciding which golf course they'll play on next. Band managers must stay close and involved with their artists, constantly advising and guiding them. Although there might be hundreds of people working with a successful band, from producers to stylists to merchandisers, the manager is the one person responsible for ensuring the entire structure doesn't collapse around his protégés. Louis Walsh has a natural born ability in this regard.

"When you think about it, the manager is the one person in the music industry that has to know everything; everything that his artist needs to do to be a success," says Fisher. "Every area in the industry involves the artist, from publishing to copyright law to record shops. The manager has to know about contract law to do with contracts for his artists. They always have lawyers and business advisers, of course, but he has to wade through that and represent his artist in those negotiations. He has got to know about the charts and how they work. He's got to understand about insurance because every time the artist goes on tour with equipment or every time it rains in the middle of a gig, he's got to be able to understand all that and know how it goes. He's got to understand about merchandising. It really is endless."

So endless, in fact, that the list of Louis Walsh's responsibilities doesn't stop there. "He needs to be an amateur psychiatrist, he really does. Artists are not always straightforward people and somebody has to talk them through their problems and troubles, so he has to understand personalities . . . and personality disorders, come to that."

While Fisher's list of a manager's responsibilities might seem exhaustive, it isn't. According to *The MMF Guide to Professional Band Management,* the official bible of music management, pop managers also have to be capable of dealing with agents, accountants, backing musicians, producers, promoters, publicists, publishers, record company executives, songwriters, sound engineers, tour managers, video directors, and any number of assistants trailing around after each of those people.

Niall Stokes, founder and editor of *Hot Press,* Ireland's leading music magazine, believes Louis always had the necessary qualities to be a successful music manager. "What he brought to the party was an obsessive love of music, an ability to inveigle people into doing things or taking a chance, a certain kind of canniness, which was an important factor for people involved in the showband scene, and an instinct for what would travel, would sell. And obviously that's a fairly substantial set of assets to set out with."

Simon Napier-Bell, former manager of Wham, Japan, and the Yardbirds among others, and author of several books on the music industry, *You Don't Have to Say You Love Me* (1982) and *Black Vinyl, White Powder* (2001), says Louis has reached the prime position in the music industry by simply finding "successful artists". He repeats the words without elaboration. He doesn't attribute the success of Louis' career as a pop svengali to anything else.

Well-known record producer Pete Waterman believes his Irish friend and business associate is driven by his love of pop music. "That sounds an obvious qualification but it is sadly lacking in most of the managers. Many of the managers today don't care about the music. They only care about the business and doing a great deal. There're a lot of guys love the deal, but don't love the music. To them, they might as well be selling carrots or bars of soap. They don't care who they're dealing with, and don't get too close to their artists or their problems."

While music critics often frown at the mention of Waterman's name and dismiss the sort of music he produces as itself no more exciting than carrots or bars of soap, his pedigree as a pop svengali can't be ignored. He has been a DJ, a record producer, a promoter, a song-writer, and a manager. He has worked with most forms of popular music from reggae to disco, and dealt with a staggering range of acts. He has also been, and still is, involved with many of Louis Walsh's acts. Waterman is a huge fan of Louis Walsh and his style of management. He attributes Louis' meteoric rise in the music industry to old-fashioned values.

"Louis Walsh is a typical example of an old-fashioned manager," opines Waterman. "I use that in a complimentary way, not in a derisory way; he's old-fashioned. He still allows his heart to rule his head and he's still more interested in the hit than making a bob. He'll make a bob but it's more important for Louis to have the hit. He'll sacrifice a lot for that hit, which is what a good manager should always do. It's old-fashioned in this day and age. Some don't give a shit about anything but how much money they can plausibly get out of it, which is why, of course, managers don't last five minutes. The minute their act isn't successful, they're gone, they're doing something else."

The fact that most pop band managers "don't last five minutes" is not just because they're obsessed with money. It's because they think they can follow the pop band formula, but they don't have the golden touch, the nous to make it happen, that special svengali quality. Louis Walsh has such a straight-forward style that many believe it is easy to emulate but there is no simple formula for pop success. To a large extent, he is misunderstood by both his critics and those who desperately want to become his protégés.

To be a pop svengali, you have to be hard-working and determined, dedicated and committed. You have to be charming and good at dealing with people. You have to be single-minded and capable of making tough decisions. You have to be able to cope with unending abuse and condescension from the critics, and an unerring talent for self-publicity certainly won't go astray. Somewhere deep inside, you have to have a hunger for power and wealth and fame. Above all else, you need a genuine love of music and a desire to make hits.

"Nobody that makes hits is admired anywhere. We've all got leprosy because we're populists," says Waterman. "We entertain the masses. Certainly for the last 20 years, it has been unacceptable socially to be populist. Everybody tries to be trendy. Well, Louis Walsh and people like him, will never be trendy ever, because unless the audience is applauding, we don't play. Critics being nice about you is smashing but we'd rather take the applause in the auditorium. Record sales are a nice bonus but the money is not what we do it for; it's the applause."

1

FROM KILTIMAGH TO DUBLIN

Louis Walsh has always considered his life outside work a private affair and the business of no one but his immediate family and those he loves. He has always done his utmost to keep his personal life to himself, apart from providing slight details about his youth during interviews. To date, there have been dozens of articles and profiles written about his life and career, but these have rarely separated the truth from the myth. He is a man shrouded in celebrity, yet he manages to evade any media intrusion.

The true story of Louis Walsh begins in the west of Ireland. Michael Louis Vincent Walsh was born on 9 August 1952 in Kiltimagh, a village situated in the heart of Mayo, a poverty-stricken county decimated by emigration since the Irish Famine of the 1840s. He was named after his father, Michael Francis, a solid man known to his friends as Frank. Louis inherited his enduring work ethic from his father, a man who worked hard and provided well for his family. From his mother Mary Catherine, known to everyone as Maureen, Louis received his unerring determination and self-belief.

The Walsh family lived on Chapel Street, the continuation of Kiltimagh's Main Street. When Louis was born, his parents already had a young daughter called Evelyn. The family was to grow considerably in the following years, with the addition of another daughter, Sarah, and six more sons: Paul, Frankie, Eamonn, Padraig, Joseph and Noel.

These days, Kiltimagh is a pretty and pleasant place to visit. The houses are gaily painted in bright pinks, greens, yellows, reds, and blues. There is a sculpture park, a museum, and retreats where artists can work.

In 1952 life was different. The village was located in part of Mayo's notorious Black Triangle, a remote hinterland where good agricultural land was scarce, and industry non-existent. East Mayo did not even get electricity until the late 1950s.

Times were hard, but Frank and Maureen Walsh did everything possible to give their children a good upbringing. Louis says his parents were "just honest hard-working people that got on very well and looked after all the kids, and that's all they ever wanted." When Louis was a child, Frank Walsh worked as a hackney driver and ran a small farm adjoining the town. Louis often had to help out on the farm but he never enjoyed it. The work was gruelling and as the family had no farm machinery, everything had to be done by hand.

His father was a quiet but authoritative figure, who never drank and held traditional values. It was an era when people worked hard to make ends meet, and raised their children to be well-mannered, polite to their neighbours, and respectful to the Catholic Church.

Louis' mother was a sociable woman who loved music and learning, and adored her children. She was particularly fond of her eldest son, who took after her in every way. "Louis was more like my mother than my father," says his brother, Frank Walsh. "She was probably the dominant person in the family."

Maureen Walsh acknowledges that Louis resembles her physically, but modesty prevents her from taking credit for his seemingly unending determination.

Both Louis' parents came from East Mayo, so the children had dozens of relations living nearby. "The front door," says Frank Walsh, "was always open. It was never locked at all. There were always loads of people in and out of the house. Of course, my father was a hackney driver as well, and there would always be people coming in and out looking for lifts here and lifts there," he said.

When Louis was a young child, his father's mother also lived in the house. "She adored the ground he walked on and he loved her too. They called her Muddy, and she was a lovely lady. She adored him and he was so fond of her. He was so upset the night she died. He must have been about 12," remembers Maureen Walsh.

Although Louis' parents provided him with proper guidance and discipline, they did not have the means to indulge their children extravagantly. The Walsh family was working class. As in most farming families of the time, the children made do with what they had and never realised the family was not materially well off. "We didn't know", says Louis and smiles. "I thought we were having a fantastic time."

As the family home was a small end-of-terrace house, the children had to share both bedrooms and beds.

"There used to be three of us in the bed, and I used to have to be in the middle," recalls Frank Walsh. "I always remember on a hot night, you could be trying to toss and turn, and someone would give you a kick."

In spite of their straitened circumstances, the Walsh children were happy and content, although Louis, in particular, could be mischievous at times.

One of his brother Frank's earliest memories is of Louis showing him how to earn money. "He used to have myself and my brother out hunting for old glass Cidona bottles, the big flagons, and the Lucozade bottles. We would gather them from the highways and byways and you could get money back on them in the shop," he recalls.

Louis' business acumen was already blossoming and he instructed his younger brothers to do the hard work, cutting their fingers on briars and bushes fishing bottles out of ditches and fields, while he took charge of the enterprise. "He would take the lion's share," remembers Frank Walsh. Louis already enjoyed the thrill of earning his own money.

With so many children in the Walsh house, it was always a loud and lively place. It is difficult to imagine the influences that shaped Louis' life and encouraged him on a career path into the music industry. His parent's example was certainly a major contributing factor. "We were a very musical house. His father was very musical and was a very good singer," says his mother.

"I haven't a note in my head at all, but I come from a musical family. My father was very into music. The love of music was on both sides of the family. When he was a child, he was very quiet but very into music from a very young age. It was all he wanted to do, was listen to music, even when he was very small," she says.

Maureen Walsh's favourite singer was Nashville star Jim Reeves, but his father preferred musicals. Louis constantly listened to his parent's musical collection on a record player given by his aunt to his father.

"I can still see it. My Aunt Anne bought it for my father when he was very sick and there were like 12 albums, *My Fair Lady, Carousel, Mario Lanza,* that type of music. It was great to have a record player then, and we used to buy 45's in Castlebar," Louis says.

Music became his drug. Music drove Louis to distraction, and he would do whatever was necessary to start collecting his own records. "I used to go into Castlebar and buy one or two. I would nick them now and again as well," he admits.

As a child who loved music so avidly, he was also glued to the radio whenever possible. He would tune it to 208 medium-wave, or as the resident DJs called it, "Radio Luxembourg – Your Station of the Stars".

Sunday nights were a particular favourite, when Jimmy Saville and Barry Aldiss played the week's top 20 hits. He was an avid reader of *Spotlight*, the top Irish pop music magazine of the day, and pored over articles about all his favourite stars. When there was no music playing at home, Louis would go across the street to a neighbour's house and sit in on the rehearsals of a local band.

Around this time, Ireland was undergoing a seismic social and cultural change. In comparison to the drab and dour 1950s, the 1960s were a whirlwind of music, dancing, and romance. As a young child, Louis was captivated by what became known as the showband era. He was young, impressionable and like all young boys, craved heroes and a sense of individuality. Louis' heroes were singers and musicians.

"One of the first records I bought was definitely *The Hucklebuck*," he says. "Evelyn and myself; we used to dance to that in our house at home. I bought the

Rolling Stones. I remember buying *Here Comes The Night* and *Let's Get Together* by Hayley Mills. And there was a Beach Boys song called *Do It Again.*

"We used to swap records down the town with different people. 45's were the big thing. They were 7/6d then or something, which was a lot of money for a poor family in Mayo."

Louis attended Kiltimagh Boys National School. He was a bright child who displayed an irreverence for authority and who always had something to say. His brother Frank remembers him making a wise crack at a bishop's expense; something his parents and contemporaries wouldn't dream of even considering.

"When the Bishop was coming around to check out the schools for Confirmation, there happened to be some-body in the class, who said they didn't believe in God. Louis puts his hand up and said, 'Don't be daft'." The story sounds implausible but is absolutely true.

When he completed his primary education, he was sent to St. Nathy's boarding school in Ballaghaderreen, Co. Roscommon to begin his secondary education. He was 11 years old.

St. Nathy's was an imposing institution that had originally been a British military barracks. The school itself had produced large numbers of priests and several bishops, which is partly why Maureen Walsh decided to send him there. She privately harboured ambitions that Louis might devote himself to the Catholic Church. He had already served as an altar boy in the local church for some years, and the family had an amicable relationship with the local clerics in the Kiltimagh parish.

If Maureen Walsh hoped her son would join the priesthood, she was mistaken. Louis hated the school. He had no intention of devoting his life to religion. He couldn't fathom why his mother expected him to enter the priesthood and take a vow of celibacy.

"My mother thought, at one stage, I might be a priest. I have no idea why. I hated the place," says Louis. "I didn't like arithmetic and geography and Latin and all that. I liked science and I liked English. It was absolutely dreadful."

Academia was lost on Louis. He was not the studious type. He resented the formality of boarding school, and did not enjoy obeying orders or bowing to ultimatums. It was a joyless time for him. Louis didn't complain about the school but accepted his predicament. But his experiences there left him depressed. His parents didn't realise how much he hated the school until he failed his first set of exams. He could find no way of fitting in, no matter how much he tried.

"I didn't realise for about a year. We always thought, 'Oh, he'll settle. He'll get used to it' but he didn't really," says his mother. In truth, Louis' mother had no other option but to send him to St. Nathy's. The reason was simple and obvious, as she explains: "You couldn't do your Leaving Certificate in Kiltimagh at that time."

But he used his time at St. Nathys to learn hard lessons about life. Reminiscing on this period, he says: "Going to boarding school . . . the food was horrible. If I had kids, I don't think I would send them to boarding school. It's like being on religious retreat all the time. I wasn't lonely, but there was no music, there was no television – the things I like. There was no good food, there was nothing. It was either Gaelic football or studying, and I had no interest in either; none at all. But I think it was good for me in one sense because it prepared me for the big bad world."

21

Although he was probably far brighter and more astute than he realised, he did not succeed academically. He failed to pass his Intermediate Certificate, the compulsory national exam for 15 year-olds. After that experience, his mother decided not to send any of her children to St. Nathy's. Louis eventually completed his education at St. Patrick's College in Swinford, nine miles from his home in Kiltimagh.

Of St. Nathy's, he says, "I left the school because I failed almost everything in my Inter Cert. They advised my mother not to send me back. I wasn't expelled. So I went to day school in Swinford. That was great fun, because I used to go down on the bus every day, having a great laugh, great fun and I got my Leaving Cert."

Louis Walsh was different from his school contemporaries in many respects. Along with having no interest in his studies, he was also uninterested in many of the passions shared by his school friends. He disliked Gaelic football, the bedrock of local life. Louis, though, had a passion of his own – pop music. He possessed an uncanny ability to remember tunes and lyrics of songs, countless songs. There was scarcely a style of popular music with which he wasn't familiar.

"All I ever wanted to do was work somehow in music. To be a DJ, or work in a radio station, or an advertising agency, or a magazine. I just wanted to work in entertainment," he says. For a youngster growing up in rural Ireland, the bright lights of show business were nothing but a far off dream. But Louis possessed both a sincere love of music and great determination, and few traits could have served him better in his ambitions to succeed in the music industry.

Pop music mesmerised Louis. He thrived on it. Music afforded him the opportunity to escape the frustration of small-town life in rural Ireland. More than anything, he wanted to be part of the music scene. At the age of 15, he got his first break.

"When I started going to St. Patrick's, I had lots of free time. I was going home every day and I wasn't studying. So I started booking this local band, a local three-piece. They were like Status Quo. They were called Time Machine."

Louis' career in the music business had begun. Soon he set about persuading more prominent band managers to give Time Machine supporting roles at concerts. As there was no telephone in the Walsh household on Chapel Street, Louis organised his fledgling business using the local phone box. He would wait anxiously outside the public telephone in Kiltimagh village until he heard it ring. He was dogged in his pursuit of securing support slots for his act.

"I used to use the local public phone box to get through to promoters like Oliver Barry, Jim Hand or Jim Aiken. They were based in Dublin. They used to give Time Machine support slots to the big showbands."

The promoters rarely met their schoolboy business associate. Instead they knew Louis by name only and were impressed by his conscientious and professional approach to his small business. Few realised how young he was because he spoke authoritatively. From Louis' perspective, this was the essence of his success. He had unlimited energy and a clever wit, which allowed him to pass himself off as someone more ex-perienced.

He also was handling more money than most of his school friends could dream of.

"We used to get £12 a night, which was fantastic money. And we would get into the gig for nothing. So we were having a great time and actually getting paid, going to the gig and meeting all the bands as well. We used to travel all over Connacht, doing supports, having a great time and I thought Time Machine were building up, getting me ready for the big time."

The money Time Machine earned was split four ways, earning Louis a tidy sum for his entrepreneurial endeavours. It was a lucrative business, considering his age. In 1967, £3 would buy you a stylish new shirt or a bundle of albums from the record shop in Castlebar.

Louis maintains the money didn't matter to him. "It was a chance for me to go and see the bands," he says. "I loved music and the showbands were brilliant."

The showbands are often ridiculed nowadays but Louis was right. They were brilliant entertainers. They brought pop music to Ireland and contributed to a major national cultural upheaval. Every weekend, people from across the class spectrum would get out on the dance floor to break the monotony of life working on farms or local businesses in rural Ireland. Louis was captivated by the industry, which he saw as dramatic and vibrant.

Before the showbands came to the west of Ireland, popular entertainment for most people hadn't changed in a century: playing cards, telling stories, and singing traditional songs. The venues where the showbands played may not have been glamourous, but the bands more than made up for this with their talent for sheer rollicking entertainment. Louis saw this ability to entertain as equally important as musical talent.

The showbands were generally made up of six to ten young men, occasionally with a woman "out front". The band members would dress in matching suits, tailored in the latest style, and all played instruments: the piano, the drums, the bass, the saxophone, the trumpet, or the trombone. Most of the showbands, however, did not play their own music.

"The showbands were judged mainly on their ability to reproduce the hits of the day, to take the top 20 and reproduce it," explains John Coughlan, the author of a book on the era. "If they could reproduce it almost exactly, they were geniuses. Not many of them showed any great originality."

Not only did the showbands sing, they also performed comedy routines. The bands toured constantly, and played six nights a week, taking only Mondays off. In the mid-sixties, it was estimated that there were 450 ballrooms in Ireland and 600 showbands travelling up and down the country. Few of these bands ever played to empty halls. The bands would play for up to four hours, with a break in the middle when a smaller relief act would take to the stage and continue to entertain the crowd.

Louis quickly learned about the dynamics of the industry and the business of entertainment. He saw how people would think nothing of driving 50 or 60 miles to see one of their favourite singers perform. He was also enthralled by the showbands. He saw them as bringing excitement, glamour, and most of all, pop music to rural Ireland.

His personal favourite was the Royal Blues Showband, an ensemble formed in May 1963 in Claremorris, eight miles from his hometown of Kiltimagh. The band's lead singer was Doc Carroll, who became famous after his band produced a No. 1 hit in the Irish charts in 1966 with *Old Man Trouble*. A year or two later, the Royal Blues provided Louis with his first proper job.

Frank and Vincent Gill were two brothers who played with the Royal Blues. In 1968, the brothers decided to make use of their musical earnings and bought a pub in Claremorris, naming it *The Blues Inn*. The Gill brothers knew the Walsh family and whenever the brothers cycled into Kiltimagh, they would leave their bicycles in the Walsh's backyard on Chapel Street.

"There were always bicycles there," says Maureen Walsh, "and they were always taken, and used for going for spins here, there and everywhere."

When the brothers bought the pub in Claremorris, Maureen Walsh inquired as to whether they could give Louis a summer job. Partly to keep Louis out of mischief for his mother's sake and partly because they needed a bar boy, the brothers agreed.

Louis didn't particularly enjoy working in the Blues Inn but he was still riotously happy. He was earning money and organising concerts for Time Machine. He had escaped the spells of anxiety and depression that had affected him in St. Nathy's. It was perhaps the closest that any youngster in Kiltimagh could come to finding a perfect life.

His love of pop was readily apparent to anyone who knew him. "The other thing I remember about him in the bar was that they used to play country and Irish music, sort of mellow music for the customers, and the minute their backs were turned, Louis would be up and he'd put on some pop, very loud pop," recalls one regular Blues Inn patron.

As Louis' passion for pop was readily evident, so was his flair for business. The wages he earned working in the pub were invested into advertising Time Machine. He had a long-term approach to everything. "Any bit of pocket money he got from working in the bar or whatever, he'd use it to buy blank paper and crayons, and spend ages doing up posters for the band, Time Machine," says one friend.

Through his work in the bar, he also got to know the Royal Blues, and started to do a little work for them too. The band had a secretary who worked out of an office in the village of Claremorris. Louis would join her to help out, taking care of the fan club and answering letters. He was in an exalted position for a teenage boy, because he also got to attend many of the Royal Blues concerts, travelling with Doc Carroll in his car. He soon developed a very good and friendly relationship with Carroll. The people he met during his formative years had an overwhelming influence on the young teenager.

The band's manager Andy Creighton played a particular role in teaching Louis about show business.

"He was ahead of his time," recalls Louis. "He would have been an amazing manager if he was around now, and he would be a very good role model to look up to. He was just an aggressive guy who got the Royal Blues to the top of the charts. He just believed and he hyped."

Louis learned about determination and getting things done by watching Creighton at his work.

"He was like a Colonel Parker. He was one of the great managers that I have known in my lifetime. Not only did he manage the Blues, he also booked their gigs and he looked after them."

Louis was lucky because he entered show business at the beginning of an era when the music scene was undergoing a metamorphosis in Ireland. There was old-fashioned music and there was pop. Pop music was the teenager's main preoccupation.

His parents, however, had grave reservations about Louis tagging along with the Royal Blues. "He'd be out all night, and he'd have to go to school in the morning," says his mother. "That didn't go down very well in the house! That was it but there was nothing you could do about it only go along with it.

"If he decided he was doing something, he did it and that was it. But actually, he never did give any problems. I'd say there are different sets of problems you'd get with teenagers, but looking back on it there was never any big problem with Louis. He didn't like drink and he didn't like smoking.

"They were two things he had an instant dislike for. Long before smoking became unpopular, he wouldn't allow it."

Doc Carroll watched Louis turn into an adult. He knew Louis would never become a farmer or settle down in Co. Mayo as would have been expected of him, but would inevitably seek a career in the entertainment industry.

"He loved pop music. He loved show business. You could see it, even then, that Louis was always going to go places," says Carroll.

According to Carroll, Louis could not hide his admiration for Creighton. He said Louis watched Creighton's every move. He made it his business to find out more. He had a high degree of curiosity about event management. Louis watched the interaction between the bands, the roadies, the managers and the ballroom owners. He saw the music trade from the inside out. In some instances, he got noticed simply because he was so young and worked hard.

Ronnie McGinn was a promoter who organised entertainment nights in the Municipal Hall in Kinsale, Co. Cork. He remembers seeing a school boy at Royal Blues concerts.

"We used to have the Royal Blues Showband down every two or three months. The thing that struck me about them was the young chap that was with them, which was Louis. I'd say he was still probably going to school. He was the road manager, as such, helping with the gear. I always thought he looked really young," says McGinn. "It was actually noticeable."

While Louis learned his trade with the Royal Blues, he was itching to try his hand full-time in the business. Once he completed his schooling, his literal escape from the small-town life of Kiltimagh was inevitable. When he got the opportunity to move to Dublin, he took it.

2

BRIGHT LIGHTS, BIG CITY

L ouis had long believed that he could forge a
successful career in the music industry, given the
chance. His parents frowned on this notion but
Louis had inherited his parent's determination and his
resolve would not be shaken. All he had ever wanted
was to leave Kiltimagh and follow his dreams. Like all
teenagers, he wanted the freedom to live his own life
without having to answer to his parents or teachers.

As soon as he had finished school, Louis went to live
in Dublin, where he continued working for the Royal
Blues Showband. Unfortunately, Doc Carroll left the
band not long after, and the Royal Blues started to
disintegrate. Having run to Dublin at the earliest
opportunity, Louis was about to be jobless in the big
city. He had no intention of returning to Kiltimagh so
he turned to his mentor, Doc Carroll, for help.
Although Carroll wasn't a big star, he was a great
entertainer with a good reputation in the music
industry. He was happy to use his influence to help his
affable young friend.

Tommy Hayden Enterprises, a Dublin-based artist
management firm, had taken over the management of
the Royal Blues in 1969. Carroll knew Hayden
personally and asked him if he would interview Louis
for a job. Hayden was bemused at the notion of a

youngster from Co. Mayo wanting a job in show business.

He remembers the conversation vividly. "Doc Carroll said to me, 'We've this young fella down here.'

"I said, 'Who is he?'

"'He's a young groupie that hangs around with us. Everywhere we go, he seems to be there. He's managing a little band called Time Machine. I thought that maybe you might give him a break,' said Doc.

"Nine times out of ten, I'd say no, but then out of the blue, he says to me, 'He's from Kiltimagh.'

"I didn't want some smart ass from the city trying to tell me what to do. I eventually met him and I liked his attitude and so forth and I said, 'Look, start when you want, then.'

"'What'll I do?' he said.

"I said, 'Well, first of all, we'll get you to do a bit of publicity here and we'll get you to make the tea and generally do things about the office'," Hayden recalls.

"He used to come up to me every night at 6 or 7 o'clock before I'd leave and say hello and say 'What should I do now?' So I would just go through all the bits and pieces with him."

The story of the small-town boy who goes in search of fame and fortune in the big city is an old one, but that doesn't make it any less exciting when you're the protagonist. Not only had he succeeded in escaping the straitened atmosphere of small-town life, but he had also secured a job working with his beloved showbands.

Now that Louis had a full-time job with Tommy Hayden, he moved to Dublin permanently. His sister Evelyn invited him to live with her. It was 1970.

"I was living with Mary, my friend from Kiltimagh," recalls Evelyn "and Louis moved in with us in our grotty little place in Ranelagh." Louis' unofficial tenancy in the flat didn't last long.

"The landlady didn't want men at all in the place. Louis would start work later than us. One day, she came checking and he was in the bath. He flew into the wardrobe but she was really cute. He had the heater plugged in and he plugged it out but she knew that somebody was after plugging out the heater. So she caught him redhanded, naked in the wardrobe! So we had to move out of that place."

Meanwhile, a great friendship developed between Louis and his new boss. Louis was like a surrogate son to Hayden while Louis held Hayden in great esteem. Hayden describes his young apprentice as a conscientious employee who quickly became schooled in the ways of the music industry. Louis respected Hayden as a self-made man who worked hard and succeeded in this demanding and competitive business.

Hayden had played the saxophone and clarinet with the Nevada Showband. He eventually became the manager of the Nevada and set up his own company, which mushroomed into one of the most respected artist management firms in Ireland. He was also very pleased with his new employee.

"I liked his demeanour and his whole attitude to life," says Hayden. "He was just like 'Yes, yes, yes, whatever you want, yes Sir, no Sir, three bags full, Sir.' He'd do anything and I just generally liked him and I can honestly say that in all the years we worked together, we never had a row. We might have agreed to disagree on something but we never had a row. It's a business made up of rows because you have to fight your corner to try and get your fees, and try and do as well as you can for your artist, but I must say we never had a row."

While the big stars played in rural venues, Dublin was the really happening place, with a greater concentration of stars performing on a more regular basis. Louis loved city life although he had little money and was sleeping on the floor of his sister's flat. As far as he was concerned, he had stepped onto the first rung of the showbusiness ladder.

"I got to really like Dublin. We didn't have a lot of money but it was great fun just to be there. Working in Tommy Hayden's office, you could go to the show-bands every night of the week. You could go out wherever you wanted for free and have a really good time. I used to go to Captain America's when it opened first. That was one of the great, great spots to go to."

Louis was firmly dedicated to his job and was certain of his future in the business. His parents were not so sure. Although their son was modestly successful in his new position, they were concerned that the job offered no long-term security. They saw a career in showbusiness as unreliable and transitory and were keenly aware that he was unqualified for any other work. If Tommy Hayden Enterprises were to suffer a decline in fortunes, he would be the first casualty.

"We didn't know how long it would go on," remembers Maureen Walsh. "It's very uncertain work, as you know, and we were thinking of something more nine-to-five. But he really worked hard. No one was going to change his mind."

His brother Frank believes Louis' early career caused his parents much anxiety. "My mother was always waiting for him to get a proper job. 'This lad won't last and what's he going to do and all that.' He just stuck at it. I don't think there was ever any question in his mind that he would ever do anything else," says Frank Walsh.

Louis was loving his new life in the city, but he still remained in constant contact with his family at home. He would travel to Kiltimagh whenever he could afford to, taking with him parcels of clothes and gifts for his younger brothers and sister.

"We used to always look forward to him coming down from Dublin," says Frank. "He always had old clothes, or excess clothes, which were probably out of date in Dublin, but which would have been terribly modern in Kiltimagh. So we thought we were the bees knees although maybe we weren't. I suppose it was the Irish version of the parcel from America."

The work in Tommy Hayden's office was only glamourous by association. Louis was a messenger boy. Hayden had hired him to help his overworked personal assistant, Carol Hanna. Not only was she dealing with the administration of Hayden's business, she was also helping Connie Lynch, another artist manager, who shared Hayden's office. Louis was hired to lessen her workload.

"I remember going in and meeting Carol Hanna and I knew she was thinking, "Who is this? What am I going to do with this guy?'" says Louis, "She was like Tommy's Girl Friday. She did everything."

Louis answered the telephones, he made the tea, he organised the cleaning and ironing of the bands clothes, and he dealt with fan mail. The work might seem menial, but Louis found it all very exciting. The office was on Hawkins St. in Dublin's city centre and it was constantly busy.

"It was like a big, big buzz there," he says. "The phones would be ringing non-stop with promoters around the country, newspapers, fans, everything. It was a real buzz."

The office was open all hours to accommodate the demands of bands, promoters and the media. Carol worked during the day while Louis took the night shift.

"I finished at half five or six o'clock, Louis would sit there and take over the office from that time until about nine or ten; that's how he got into the routine of working mainly evenings. During the day, he would come in to me around 2 p.m. and he would do different things that we would need him to do.

"Sometimes he would have to go to London to collect suits for the band, sometimes he'd be doing general things for me and helping me. After 6 p.m. he looked after and managed his own band Time Machine. That was his little bonus for doing a bit of the office work and helping out, he managed his own band then in the evening," says Carol.

Carol and Louis quickly became firm friends. She was protective of Louis, treating him almost like a little brother, and he looked up to her.

"Louis and myself bonded from the start. I used to look after him, did everything for him, all through the years. Louis and I were like best of friends, best of buddies. We had our hot moments, we had our fiery moments and we'd roar. He's Cancerian and I'm Leo and there's a bit of a clash there in our personalities," she says.

"But Louis and I were like brother and sister. We'd be fighting one minute and the next minute, he would ask me for a cup of coffee. That's the way it is. We'd be roaring at each other and then he would turn around and say, 'Make us a cup of coffee there, fish face.' He's fire and no patience, no tolerance. He's absolutely intolerant. He'd just go bananas and suddenly in the next minute then, he's fine. I do the same, by the way. And we worked like that."

Louis immersed himself in city life. His favourite nightspot was the Television Club, or the TV Club, on Harcourt Street.

"We used to go to the Television Club on a Monday night. All the bands would be playing there. English bands like Marmalade, the Tremeloes, but the great bands for me were the Freshmen, Chips, the Platter-men, and the Miami. They were brilliant Irish bands," says Louis.

The Television Club was lively place that attracted everyone of note from the Dublin showbusiness scene. An added bonus for Louis was that he didn't have to pay admission, as he worked for Tommy Hayden Enterprises. The club was owned by Eamonn Andrews, who would later present *This is Your Life* on UK television, and who was a major Irish celebrity. John Coughlan remembers the venue well: "For a couple of years it was the most successful venue. It also spanned the pure dance hall and the discotheque. We used to run dances there on a Monday night called the 'Spotlight Night Out'. We'd play all the big bands and visiting international acts. We'd get people like the Everly Brothers there and Roy Orbison – quite big stars. Monday night was a night off for most of the bands and they'd all gather on the balcony to see how their competitors were performing. You'd have Joe Dolan and Brendan Bowyer in to see Dickie Rock performing. It was quite a big social occasion, very glamourous."

Glamourous, and a world away from the ballrooms of East Mayo. In time, Louis got to know more about the workings of the showband business. Hayden gave him more responsibility and allowed him to book out bands himself. Along with Time Machine, which was still availing of his services, he also booked out a band from Sligo Town called Brotherly Love, an Irish version of the Cassidys.

Louis was more than fortunate in that Hayden was well known and, more importantly, well respected on the entertainment scene. From the beginning, his tenure at Hayden's company served him well. He learned about the business from the ground up: how to secure concerts for bands; haggle with ballroom owners; outmanoeuvre rival managers, and how to think on his feet. As he honed his negotiation skills, he also developed an intuition for sizing up the people with whom he dealt, and identifying those he could trust and do business with.

Hayden was a skilled promoter and was adept at persuading radio, television, and press journalists to cover his acts. Louis watched and learned and picked up publicity skills that would stand to him in later years; skills that would even gain him a certain notoriety among journalists.

Before Louis ever graduated to booking out bands, Hayden would dispatch him around the newspapers in Dublin to deliver press releases and photographs. All the time he was building up contacts in the media and in related companies.

Once he got a chance to do a little promoting of his own, he seized it with gusto. John Coughlan remembers being a frequent recipient of phone calls from Louis, when he was editor of *Spotlight*.

"He was a bit of a pest. A very tenacious, persuasive pest, but very affable. You couldn't dislike him, really," says Coughlan. "[He was] persistent, tenacious, persuasive." Thirty years later, this description is still accurate, though few in the media or music industry would dare to call him a "pest" today.

Louis' obvious ambition and enthusiasm struck a chord with Hayden. Any uncertainty that Louis had initially displayed faded away. As he settled into his job, his confidence grew.

"He would come in and say 'Tommy, I've got a great idea. What do you think about this?' I'd say to him, 'Well, maybe.'

"And then he'd say 'But, but, but, I don't mean that' and he would put it another way to me and then suddenly I would start grabbing the idea.

"He also used to come in to me with songs, playing me songs all the time. I had a band called Red Hurley, Kelly and the Nevada in those days, who were successful on the circuit here. Red had ten No. 1s. He was a household name in about 18 months and Louis used to always come in with new songs. Every second day, he would be in with new songs, saying 'I've got a great song for you.'

"I said to myself, 'this guy is definitely going places, no doubt about that'. Every second minute I saw him in the early days, when he was supposed to be working, he was reading these music magazines, bringing himself up to date," recalls Hayden.

The breadth of music on offer in Dublin was a revelation to the young man from Kiltimagh. Louis also attended every concert he could, and often stayed out all night.

"I could never get him out of bed before 5 p.m. in the evening and into the office," recalls Hayden. "Then he used to tell me, his philosophy on that one was: 'I can't get anyone until tea time,' and then also he said the phones were cheaper after 6 o'clock, so he was saving money."

Louis seized every opportunity provided by his job with Hayden's company. It was a memorable period in his life, during which he developed his business acumen and built up a network of contacts that any aspiring manager would envy. Between watching famous acts play the TV Club, and cutting deals wherever he could, Louis ingratiated himself with those at the top of the music scene. He was lucky. He found a job he loved and a mentor who knew the trade. He made great friends and important contacts.

He would soon find out, however, that there was a dark side to the bright lights of show business and the social whirl of the big city. As the 1970s progressed, it seemed that his luck was beginning to run out, as the young people of Ireland turned away from the showbands. There were hard times ahead for the young man from Kiltimagh.

The glory days of the Irish showbands did not last. The brilliance of the ballroom era was the product of an extraordinarily rich pool of musical talent drawn from all over Ireland. By the mid 1970s, however, Louis realised that the excitement that had characterised the scene in the sixties was dead and gone. Slowly he came to the conclusion that the showbands were yesterday's men. They had opened the ears of the young people of Ireland to new music as they whirled around the country but, inevitably, they had fallen out of favour as the new generation of young people were drawn to alternative styles of music: rock and disco.

"The showbands just started disappearing," says Louis. "Disco came in, nightclubs opened up and the showband scene was just phased out totally. It was a pity because they were all great at the time. Only for the showbands, I don't know where we'd be now.

"There were great stars in the showbands, people like Red Hurley, Joe Dolan and Dickie Rock. They were all great entertainers. They went out and they sang live every night. They should have been international; they could have been. But they stayed here working the circuit. They were entertainers. It was a great time in Ireland and should not be forgotten."

The audiences of the 1970s were all too keen to forget. They wanted to hear electric guitars; music inspired by Jimi Hendrix, Eric Clapton and the like. Irish bands such as Rory Gallagher and Taste, and Phil Lynott and Thin Lizzy sprang up to meet the demand. These bands were rough, mean and edgy, in contrast to the showbands, who were clean-cut, polite and harmonious. And therein lay the appeal of the rock bands. Disco was even more popular and happening, with the emphasis on uninhibited dancing and outrageous clothes.

In the mid 1970s, this was a nightmare for the agents behind the showband scene. Louis, however, understood that he had to adapt to the new diversity on the music scene. Although he understood that showbands had provided his wages, his instincts told him that music and musical tastes were about to change. He devoted his time to exploring new venues and learning about all the new types of music on offer.

Jim Aiken, who would later found the event management firm, Aiken Promotions, recalls being struck by the sheer variety of music, which appealed to the young booking agent.

"Louis and myself crossed paths when Louis was a kid from Mayo," he says.

"I remember him coming to the shows in the National Stadium. He would have been a teenager, I suppose, very early twenties. He was this guy who loved music, who knew every genre of music. He turned up at rock, he turned up at pop, he turned up at folk, he turned up at Demis Roussos, he turned up at Don MacLean, he turned up at jazz, he turned up at Moving Hearts, Led Zeppelin and Nana Mouskouri. He turned up at everything and he was always doing something in the music business himself."

Clearly, his interest in music determined the direction in which his career was heading; he was forever analysing the styles of music the public wanted. He immersed himself in various styles of music, although he rarely became a part of the culture that accompanies them. He watched rock bands but was not a rocker. He listened to disco but was not a dancer. He knew far more about popular music and its origins than most DJs. He possessed what industry sources describe as a peculiar ability to understand an audience.

He also assessed acts in terms of their overall entertainment value. Many less than extraordinary bands could enthrall an audience with a well-rehearsed play list and some nifty dance moves. He saw their stage presence and ability to entertain as being equally important as their music, in terms of bringing in an appreciative crowd of paying punters.

Louis was one of the few agents who saw the collapse of the showband industry at close quarters, and he learned valuable lessons during this time. He saw singers and musicians squander their earnings on drink and women. He witnessed their marriages breaking up and saw managers defrauding their clients. Many inexperienced musicians were caught up in the heady whirl of the showband era and neglected to keep their feet on the ground and plan for a less lucrative future. Musicians like these were destroyed by the business. Louis watched and took note.

He found working as an agent for Tommy Hayden during this period tiresome, as time and time again, ballroom promoters would attempt to defraud his acts.

Speaking on RTE Radio, he recalled the difficulties of dealing with the promoters. "Slogging around Irish ballrooms. That was the worst thing of my life. I've still got baggage from it because, you know why, because some promoters never paid. The promoters around Ireland were the worst. They had four walls and a roof and they treated the artists, the bands, like shit. And if the people didn't come out, you didn't get paid."

Hayden was wise to the demise of the showbands and moved to diversify his business interests, acquiring a number of nightclubs, while continuing to manage and book out bands. More responsibility fell on Louis, who was now a stalwart in the company.

But even if his acts drew large crowds, all of the money was taken at the door of the ballroom. There were no tickets and no accounts, so it was easy to rip off a young band and its young booking agent. If the band didn't get paid for a gig, he didn't get his 10 percent booking fee. As the industry went into free fall, some ballroom managers became even more untrustworthy and desperate. Sometimes some of the bands and their managers tried to rip him off. In the midst of all the wheeler dealing, he discovered the booking agent inevitably came off the worst.

To his credit, Louis was regarded as a professional, who watched out for his bands. He knew when to make demands and when to walk away. He realised an agent had no control unless he could play the game. He understood how important it was to keep the ballroom owners mollified, if his acts were to play in their venues again. Furthermore, well-connected ballroom owners could arrange gigs for the show-bands in Las Vegas and other US cities. These tours usually took place during March and April; months that coincided with the onset of Lent, a time when the local social scene slowed considerably.

Although he was light years ahead in terms of his grasp of music and trends in entertainment, he was still young and relatively inexperienced in his job. Even when no-one was trying to rip him off, the young Louis struggled at times. He was young and relatively inexperienced in his job and spent his days dealing with crafty ballroom owners and promoters who were past masters at emerging on the better end of deals. With time, however, he learned to decipher the body language of deceit and pick up on any hints of skull-duggery. By the time the showband industry was in its final stages of collapse, he had become more than adept at bargaining.

Donal Maguire, who used to book acts from Tommy Hayden Enterprises for the annual Festival of the Carberys in Leap, Co. Cork, recalls that Louis was no fool. "You'd have to bargain with him, of course. If there was a band that wasn't doing very well, you might have to take them as well as the crowd you really wanted."

Virtually everyone who worked in the music industry at the time says he was a very reliable person. People still regard him as, perhaps, the most honest agent they ever dealt with during that period. Like all agents, he wanted to earn money, but he understood that it was a three way relationship between the band, booking agent and dance hall owner. He had intuitive knowledge of the workings of the business. He saw it as risky, even foolhardy, to mess people around. For his reliability and personal commitment, he was trusted.

"All his bands would turn up," says Maguire, in a tone that implied that acts booked with other agents weren't always such a safe bet. "What you said went. He'd never let you down. The bands would always turn up. I remember we had booked Johnny Logan to do the festival in 1980 and he still showed up in August, even though he had won the Eurovision a few months earlier."

During the 1970s, Louis continued to book out big name showbands such as Billy Brown and the Freshmen; a band noted for their ability to perfectly reproduce the sound of the Beach Boys, and Red Hurley and the Nevada. Newer showband-style cabaret acts such as Rob Strong and the Plattermen, and Linda Martin and Chips were also on his books as were, from time to time, rock acts including such luminaries as Thin Lizzy and The Horslips.

By 1976, most of the big name showbands had vanished, splintered and fallen apart. By the end of the decade, they were gone for good. Some of the showbands lead singers, such as Brendan Bowyer, Dickie Rock, and Joe Dolan, adapted their talents to cabaret, and continued to perform.

The entertainment industry in Ireland had changed completely. Louis found the transition difficult. Finding wealth and success proved an even more elusive goal. He secured plenty of work, although he didn't always get paid for it. From Louis' point of view, it was just a means to an end. He was making a living and enjoying life to a certain extent but he was no longer immersed in pop music.

All in all, the 1970s were not a good time for Louis Walsh. By the end of the decade, he had no money and was no nearer to finding success in the music business. The daily drudgery of dealing with rock bands had left him disillusioned, but he stuck with it because it was better to be miserable on the inside of the business than to be miserable away from it, and wishing he was still involved. Furthermore, he wasn't qualified for any other career.

3

WHAT'S ANOTHER YEAR?

When Louis was growing up in Co. Mayo, the showbands were not the only musical phenomenon that interested him. The Eurovision Song Contest also caught his imagination. This annual carnival of pop began in 1956, but it was not until 1965 that Ireland entered the Contest for the first time. Butch Moore, the lead singer of the Capitol Showband, represented his country in Naples performing *Walking the Streets in the Rain*, and finished in sixth place.

Luxembourg took the prize that year with Poupée de Cire, Poupée de Son, a song composed by Serge Gainsbourg. Moore may not have won but his limited success in Naples was treated as an outstanding achievement when he returned to Ireland.

In Kiltimagh, a 12-year-old boy who loved pop music was enthralled by the hysteria surrounding Moore, and became hooked on the Eurovision Song Contest. Louis loved the Eurovision and regarded it as one of the most important nights of the year.

"I used to watch the Eurovision when I was growing up and I remember watching Sandie Shaw and Dana and all these people. When we were in school, it was the big, big show of the year. What a big show!

"It was the biggest music show in the world. Looking back now, it was kitsch and very naff, but there were some great singers in it then. They would just put in the best singer from Ireland, whoever was No. 1, like Dickie Rock or Butch Moore. In England, they had Cliff Richard and Olivia Newton John. It was the best singers and the best songs," says Louis.

In 1979, the Eurovision was a legitimate musical and business enterprise, and Irish artists regarded it as a great opportunity to boost their careers. Through his work with Tommy Hayden Enterprises, Louis had met many singers and musicians who would do anything to succeed, but few who possessed the capability, talent and stamina worthy of international acclaim. A chance meeting on a bus heading from Dublin City to Co. Kildare was to change all that.

"I met Johnny Logan on a bus going down to Goffs in Co. Kildare," he recalls. "He was doing 'Joseph and the Technicolour Dreamcoat'. He told me he was with Jim Hand (another well-known artist manager) and I said 'I'd love to manage you'."

Logan's real name was Seán Sherrard. He was already signed to Hand and had achieved some success in the Irish National Song Contest, the stepping-stone to the Eurovision. Sherrard had been an electrician since he left school, but had also been singing in concerts since the age of 14, influenced by his father, a well-known Irish tenor who performed as Patrick O'Hagan. It was a common occurrence in those days to take a stage name.

Logan had performed his own song *Angie* in the 1979 National Song Contest and came a credible third, but it didn't help his career much. He continued working as a jobbing singer, travelling around Ireland in his blue Fiat Mirafiore to concerts staged in provincial towns.

When Louis met Logan on the bus, he immediately spotted his potential and acted quickly to initiate a management deal.

Working through Tommy Hayden Enterprises, Louis negotiated a deal with Hand whereby both companies would earn money if anything ever became of Logan's career. Hand signed a contract with Tommy Hayden Enterprises on 13 March 1979, making Hayden's company the sole management and promoters for the singer, while Hand would continue to receive his 10 percent for a further two years. Louis was the driving force behind the deal. Hand hadn't much hope of success for Logan but he knew it would be foolhardy to sign away all potential earnings from the singer to Tommy Hayden.

Under Louis' guiding hand, Logan's career blossomed for a time, driven by Louis' belief that Logan was a rare talent.

"I just thought he was young and a great artist, a great middle of the road singer," says Louis. "I think he was a fantastic singer and a fantastic performer at the time, and he was different to everybody else. Looking back on it, he was streets ahead of anyone who's around at the moment."

Louis wasn't the only good omen to cross Logan's path. Another unexpected boost came when Logan met Shay Healy, who worked as a press officer with RTE, the national broadcaster. Healy was also a songwriter and one of his compositions was to prove the catalyst that launched Logan's career into a higher orbit. After the death of Healy's mother, he had written a song called *What's Another Year* for his father. On meeting Johnny and hearing him sing, he thought his song would suit Logan's style perfectly.

The song itself had been rejected for entry into the Castlebar International Song Contest that year, but Healy had faith in it, and persuaded Logan to sing it in the following year's National Song Contest. Louis was happy for Johnny to have a go at the Eurovision but he didn't like Healy's song.

"He gave us this song called *What's Another Year*. I heard it. I said it was awful," he says. "I did think it was awful, but I said: 'It's a TV show. Let's do it. It's going to be promotion.'

"That's the way I looked at things at the time. Shay Healy got Bill Whelan to do an amazing arrangement, he put a sax on it, and *What's Another Year* just walked the Song Contest. Johnny, overnight, was hot."

Whelan's involvement had proved crucial. He re-arranged the song, adding a saxophone introduction, which lifted it and immediately caught the listeners attention.

At the 1980 National Song Contest, held in the studios of RTE and hosted by DJ Larry Gogan, the result was never in doubt. Logan won the competition with 40 points; 19 points clear of his nearest rival. Louis was still unschooled in international band management but he had brought Logan's career this far, with the backing of Tommy Hayden.

Louis made the arrangements to travel to The Hague where the 1980 Eurovision was due to take place. Although participation in the event was enormously exciting for Louis, he was unable to generate any serious media coverage. Ireland hadn't won the Contest since 1970, and few people in the music industry seemed that sure of Logan's chances.

On the day of the Contest, the *Irish Times* didn't cover Logan's participation in the Eurovision. The *Irish Independent* didn't mention Logan either, although

Kate Robbins, a member of Prima Donna, the English entry, did get a few paragraphs as she was confined to bed suffering from "a high temperature and exhaustion", and was unlikely to perform in the Contest. The *Irish Press* did report on Logan's chances, saying *What's Another Year* had emerged as a strong favourite to win the Contest, after the previous night's dress rehearsal. This information, however, was supplementary to the big Eurovision story; that the Dutch Tulip Growers Association had decided to name a new tulip after the singer of the winning entry.

Louis and the rest of Logan's entourage ran wild in The Hague. Their hotel became the social headquarters for those competing in the Eurovision. The Irish contingent threw wild and extravagant parties every night in the week leading up to the Contest.

"I was there with Tommy Hayden, Johnny Logan, Jim Hand, Thelma Mansfield and Pat Kenny. I remember Pat cycling around the foyer of the hotel on a bike. He was great fun and he was just into the whole thing and we had the best fun ever," Louis recalls.

Louis, in typical fashion, kept a beady eye on the competition during rehearsals and took comfort from any mishap that befell Logan's rivals. Both Louis and Healy were particularly worried about the Italian entry, Alan Sorrenti. As luck would have it, Sorrenti had an enormous row with his wife. "She was threatening to throw herself from the hotel window, and we thought 'Well, that's him disconcerted'," says Shay Healy.

Louis may have been worried about Logan's rivals, but he tried not to show it. He knew Logan needed all the support and protection in the run-up to the Contest.

Healy took a more direct approach. For the entire week before the Contest, he wore a sweatshirt with the words: "It is imperative that I win this contest" printed on the back.

On Saturday, 19 April 1980, Logan finally took to the stage in the 25th Eurovision Song Contest. Louis was confident; Hayden was confident and Jim Hand was about to realise he'd made a serious error of judgment. There were hundreds of people in the audience at the Congresgebouw that night and 500 million more watching the event live on television. Twenty-four-year-old Logan wasn't fazed, however, and performed with his heart.

Some singers chose to underplay emotions but Logan gave the performance his all. Juries all over Europe were touched at the sight of this boyishly handsome singer and his heartfelt song of woe.

As the close of the voting drew near, six countries had given Ireland top marks. Belgium had the deciding vote, and duly awarded their 12 points to Ireland. Logan won with 143 points, beating German entrant Katja Ebstein into second place by five points. At that precise moment, Logan made the transition from little-known local singer to global star.

Louis and Hayden felt the commercial reverberations of the win within minutes.

"Jim Hand wanted to manage him overnight. He suddenly was his best friend, even though he didn't want to know him before. He was there because legally he had Johnny under contract. He didn't care about him. He was a liability to him. Jim was a brilliant manager but he had let Johnny go," says Louis.

Louis was now handling an internationally successful artist. Logan's win was the beginning of a whirlwind of celebrity. His triumph was reported on the front pages of the Sunday and Monday news-papers around the globe, under headlines such as "What another win" and "Johnny Logan, King of Europe".

Louis was determined to use the publicity to his advantage. A rousing welcome was organised for Logan at Dublin Airport, with journalists, politicians and Aer Lingus dignitaries jostling for position on the tarmac. From the moment Logan stepped off the plane at Dublin airport, wearing white leather trousers and a black leather coat, it was clear that Logan's career had taken an immeasurable turn for the better. There were thousands of well-wishers and fans thronging the airport balconies. "When Johnny went to walk amongst them, he was totally mobbed. At one point, it even seemed mildly dangerous for him," remembers Shay Healy.

Louis stood on the sidelines with Healy and Hayden while Logan embraced his success. Louis likened the reception to Beatlemania, as he pondered how Jim Hand would react to letting such an obviously talented singer go.

Incidentally, the new Eurovision winner arrived home carrying a bunch of Johnny tulips. The Dutch Tulip Growers Association had made good on their promise.

Probably the only people not overcome by delight at Logan's Eurovision win were the organisers of the Castlebar International Song Contest, who were castigated in the newspapers for committing the "boob of a lifetime" by failing to select the song for their competition in the previous year. The contest director, David Flood, admitted to the *Irish Press*, "It was a blunder. I am sure we will hear a lot about it."

In the weeks that followed, Logan enjoyed glamour in spades. Before the win, Louis had booked him to perform at nine concerts in the 12 days following the contest, aware that life had to go on after the week of fun in The Hague. Once Logan won, however, these gigs were swiftly cancelled and Louis arranged a European tour. In the following 12 days, Logan visited Switzerland, the UK, France, Germany, the Netherlands, and Belgium, playing to packed venues.

Tommy Hayden Enterprises acted swiftly to capitalise on the win, and garner as much media coverage as possible. Louis was instrumental in planting stories in the national media about Logan, who embraced his newfound fame. On the Wednesday after the contest, he spent £522 on new clothes in London. That same night, he recorded a piece for *Top of the Pops*, where Legs & Co, the show's dancers, presented the young singer with a giant birthday cake. The producers placed him in the final slot before the No. 1 single, indicating their belief that *What's Another Year* would soon reach No. 1. Louis was in the studio too, keeping in the background and soaking up the atmosphere. For him, *Top of the Pops* was the pinnacle of pop. It was his first taste of international success, and an amazing break from the grind of booking out small-time acts back home.

Top of the Pops wasn't the only high profile television show where Logan appeared. On the Friday night, he appeared on the *Late Late Show,* where he was presented with a new Talbot Salara, a car that wasn't even on the market yet. The following night, he appeared on British television again, appearing on the *Val Doonican Show*. Princess Beatrix of Holland contacted Tommy Hayden Enterprises the next week asking if it was possible for Logan to sing at her coronation ball. Logan duly obliged, saying: "Who am I to refuse a Queen?".

Tommy Hayden and Louis watched Logan carefully. He was fast turning into an international star. His single surpassed all of their expectations. *What's Another Year* sold half a million copies within three days of its release, catapulting Logan to No. 1 in 11 European countries, including Ireland and the UK.

Logan was the first male Irish singer ever to reach No. 1 in the UK singles chart, and *What's Another Year* was the first Eurovision-winning UK No. 1 since Waterloo in 1974. The song stayed at No. 1 in the UK for two weeks and ultimately sold 3 million copies.

Rapid success can be controlled, but other people's reactions to it are sometimes difficult to handle. While Logan was achieving stardom and popular acclaim beyond his wildest dreams, he was at the centre of a contractual crisis. He was entangled with two managers and five record companies.

Jim Hand had negotiated a recording contract with an Irish company called Release Records in 1975. In almost five years, Release Records released only one of his singles in France, and two or three in Ireland. None of these had performed well. Furthermore, Logan claimed Hand had paid him much less than the £100 per week he was supposed to receive. He said Hand had told him to "go get a job in Dunnes [the Irish supermarket chain]".

When Logan met Louis, he was not happy with his record company, or his manager, and wanted new representation. Although Hand had signed a contract with Tommy Hayden Enterprises making them sole management and promoters for the singer, he sought an injunction preventing Logan from working without his involvement within days of the Eurovision win. "It was the usual Irish thing. Where there's a hit, there's a writ. That's what happened," says Louis.

The dispute inevitably ended in court but was settled prior to the hearing.

"It was huge at the time," recalls Hayden. "I bore all the costs. We had done a deal with Jim because he couldn't break the guy, so he said to us 'Sure, you take him on and if you do something, sure give us a few bob and we'll be grand.'" Logan's unprecedented success meant that Hand was less than happy with "a few bob" and all concerned ended up in court. Tommy Hayden explains what happened.

"Johnny came to me in the office one day and said 'Please don't let me go back there. Please look after me here. I like what's happening here. Yourself and Louis are great. Let's stick together.' Stick together, all right. I went into court and I spent thousands, thousands. I think it ended up something like £10,000, which was an awful lot of money in those days," says Hayden.

A deal was reached, which saw Louis and Hayden emerge triumphant. Tommy Hayden and Louis Walsh were confirmed as Logan's management team, with Louis appointed as the singer's "personal manager". Under Louis' direction, Logan should have had a glittering career ahead of him. Power, success, and a few hefty managerial commission cheques should have awaited him. Except it didn't quite happen like that.

"He should have been a big, big star," says Louis. "But if I knew then, what I know now, I'm sure I would have handled things a lot differently."

Logan's contractual obligations created a labyrinth of disputes and legal obstacles. Release Records saw the opportunity presented by the Eurovision and rushed out an album of material recorded in late 1977 and 1978, along with *What's Another Year*. Release sold the UK rights of the album to Pye, but Release only had the Irish rights to *What's Another Year* so the UK album was missing this song.

Another company called Spartan Records spotted this omission and began importing the Irish version of the album into the UK at the same time. If this wasn't already a glut of record companies, Irish firm Spider Records owned the world rights and CBS (now Sony), the only global player involved, had purchased the future world rights. Deciphering which company was entitled to which rights took time to disentangle, but time was the one thing Logan did not have on his side. It was crucial for the future of his career that a strong follow-up single and an album of new material were released quickly.

As protracted negotiations started to reach agreement between the record companies involved, Logan embarked on an Irish tour in the summer of 1980. The tour, however, was over-ambitious and proved to be a disaster from a financial point of view. Tommy Hayden Enterprises was left seriously out of pocket. Logan was devastated by the failure of the tour. To make things worse, the media began to turn on him.

Four months after Logan had won the Eurovision, CBS finally released a second single called *Save Me*. It received dreadful reviews and flopped. It didn't even reach No. 100 in the charts. CBS had already spent £87,000 on Logan's album but the record company decided it was better to cut its losses and run. Logan was dropped. Louis was gutted.

The media went to town on Logan and it didn't take long for his star to fade. By Christmas 1980, he was a has-been. Instead of topping the charts again, he was appearing as Joseph in Rock Nativity in Cork Opera House.

Louis didn't see the experience as a complete failure. "Johnny became famous but he could have been a lot more famous," he says. "He had a No. 1 in 10 countries. I remember going to *Top of the Pops* with him and him singing live. Everybody loved him. The record was huge. *What's Another Year* was a huge hit record. He recorded it in Spanish, in German and everything and it's still a well-played record around the world.

"Everybody blames everybody when it doesn't work. When it works, they never praise anybody. He's had a good career, but he hasn't been as big as he should have been. At the end of the day, what really happened? I don't know. It's one of those great Irish things; everybody had an opinion on it. We were all naïve but we believed in him. Everybody can blame everybody else, but I still believe the records weren't as good as they should have been but he still had a big career, and he still does very well."

Was Louis to blame for what happened to Logan? A little, but not too much. Other factors played a part in the young singer's downfall.

Whatever mistakes Louis made in the summer of 1980, he made up for them many times over, according to friends. As Logan's career stumbled and faltered over the next decade, Louis was one of the few people in the business who stood by him

4

MR. EUROVISION

Life for Louis quickly returned to normal after his experience at the Eurovision. Logan was just one of the artists managed by Tommy Hayden Enterprises. For months after Logan's career slid into ignominy, he remonstrated with himself, wondering if he could have done things differently. In truth, he knew he had done everything possible for Logan. Any mistakes he made, were not intentional or malicious. Chastened by the experience, he went back to his day job, more determined than ever to push his artists as best he could.

For some years, Louis had been booking concerts for Linda Martin and her band Chips, and later become her manager. He was first introduced to Martin in Clogherhead, a village in Co. Louth, in the company of Tommy Hayden.

"She was singing with Lyttle People and we went up to see them," he says. "They had just left Chips, herself and Paul Lyttle, and started their own band. We took them on. They weren't doing very well and we tried everything with them, got them TV, got them records and got them working."

Despite Louis' best efforts, Lyttle People didn't really succeed and the original Chips group then got back together. The act continued to be represented by Tommy Hayden Enterprises.

Martin was an attractive redhead from Belfast. She was a talented singer and Louis believed strongly in her ability to become an international artist. He was good at assessing artists strengths and capabilities, and he sensed that Martin had what it took. More importantly, from her point of view, he believed she could be a strong contender for Eurovision success. By 1984, Martin was an experienced cabaret singer, who had been singing on the circuit for 10 years. She was also a friend of Johnny Logan's for a number of years, and when she needed a song for the Eurovision, Logan obliged. He produced a song called *Terminal 3*, which was a lament on the scourge of emigration and long-distance love.

Although Logan's star had faded after 1980, Louis still believed in the potential offered by the Eurovision. It was, he believed, one of the best opportunities for Irish singers to perform before a truly international audience. It also gave him the chance to make international media contacts.

"You had camera crews and photographers from every country around Europe, and they always wanted to talk to the Irish act for some reason. I think it's because we were politically free as well in Eurovision, and that helped it as well," he says.

Another reason Louis persisted in persuading his acts to enter the Eurovision was simply that he was a long-standing fan of the Contest. "I liked all the early Eurovision songs," he says. "I'm not shy about that. I still like a lot of them."

In 1984, the Eurovision was still a hugely popular event across Europe and Louis saw it as an opportunity that should be taken and not sneered at. Four years after Logan's win, Louis was once again bound for the Contest. *Terminal 3* won the Irish National Song Contest on 31 March 1984, narrowly beating Sheeba (who had represented Ireland at the Eurovision in 1981) into second place by two points. Martin was shocked. She had participated in the competition with her group Chips in 1976, 1977, 1978 and 1982, but had never managed to actually win it. Still, won it she had, and soon she was the pundit's favourite to win the Eurovision too.

The signs were good, as these things go. Before the Contest had even taken place, Martin had been signed up for tours of Turkey and the then Czechoslovakia later in the year. Tommy Hayden Enterprises had developed good contacts in the entertainment industry across Europe.

Luxembourg hosted the 1984 Eurovision, and most of the same people that had accompanied Logan to The Hague travelled to Luxembourg with Martin and Louis, who were now close friends. Like before, they partied the week away before the Contest, this time more quietly confident than they had been in 1980. Moments like these were some of the happiest in Louis' life. He loved the wheeling and dealing that went on behind the scenes. He was always anxious to hear news about the other acts and meet other managers. Although he enjoyed being part of the Eurovision scene, Louis had secret reservations about Martin's chances.

"I didn't think she would even be in the top three," he says, "I didn't think the song was amazing at all. I didn't think it was great but she had a brilliant image at the time with the red hair and the white clothes. It wasn't a good production but it was good for her."

Privately, he didn't believe Ireland would take the first prize having watched the other contestants perform and rehearse.

When the Saturday night arrived, the Irish team headed for the Municipal Theatre in the hope that Martin would win. She wore a white trouser suit, which was complemented by a blue sash, blue shoes, and seriously big hair. She sang well, but the song was not successful. When the voting was completed, she had 137 points, eight points less than the winners. Ignominious and annoying as it was to come second when she was so close to winning, Martin's loss was compounded by the fact that the winners were essentially a novelty act from Sweden. They were the Herreys, three brothers who turned up on stage in matching white trousers and gold boots. One wore a blue shirt, one a red shirt, and the other a turquoise shirt, so you could tell them apart. Their song was called *Diggi-Loo, Diggi-Ley*.

The Irish team were devastated not to win and understandably so. Louis, however, was character-istically chirpy and refused to be downbeat about coming second.

"I was really happy she got second," he says, "It helped her incredibly here. It was great from her point of view."

True to form, he came out fighting. On the morning after the Contest, the team sat around a table drinking coffee. Everyone was still crushed by the defeat. Except Louis. He was the only one keeping spirits up and staying optimistic. "If he had a title on the team, it would have been 'Chief Emotional Support'," recalls Healy.

He began to show the confident public persona for which he would later become known, telling the *Irish*

Press that *Terminal 3* had already been released across Europe.

"We will be pushing it by concentrating on countries that gave us 10 or 12 marks in the Contest," said Louis. "Linda was treated after the show as if she were the winner. That was the impact of her performance. There is no doubt now that she has a very big future."

Although she had TV appearances lined up in Cyprus, France, Holland, Luxembourg, Portugal and Turkey, her promotional tour wasn't accompanied by the near-hysteria that had greeted Logan everywhere he went in the weeks following his win. Neither was Martin guaranteed the influx of cash that Logan had received.

Louis was privately anxious to achieve something more after he returned to Ireland. He continued working for Tommy Hayden Enterprises, representing and managing all types of performers but he didn't like much of the music they performed.

Rock music was the only art form that mattered in Ireland in the 1980s, largely because of the success of U2. As the DJ Dave Fanning has said, it was a time "when you were either too much like U2 or too little like U2. Everything was compared to them. Pop music didn't get a look in."

If Louis loved anything, it was pop music. He gravitated naturally towards commercial music and sounds. His attitude towards Irish rock was ambivalent. The rock bands paid his wages but he never liked the music and was not enamoured by the rock scene and it's culture.

One of the artists who mattered most to him appeared to be fading into oblivion. Logan had sunk deeper into decline since the collapse of his international career in 1980. His despair was compounded when another of his songs, *Hearts,* sung by his brother Mike Sherrard, came last in the 1985 National Song Contest, garnering only three points from the unsympathetic juries around Ireland.

Louis, however, was unbowed by this disaster and exhorted Logan to give it one more try. Logan did so, writing *If I Can Change Your Mind* for Linda Martin. She performed the song in the 1986 National Song Contest, and came fourth. It seemed as if another day of Eurovision glory for Logan and Louis was not to be.

Few people have the endurance of Louis Walsh. He remained the biggest advocate of the Eurovision in Ireland and spent long hours promoting Johnny Logan and Linda Martin, according to Shay Healy. He sent out their concert posters himself, demonstrating that he was a hands on manager. Patiently, he encouraged Logan and Martin to persevere and not to accept failure. His desire for success for both himself and his friends helped make him a zealous advocate of hard work and persistence.

While Louis remained buoyant and determined, Logan was downbeat. By 1987, his career was in tatters. The journalist Orna Mulcahy wrote in the *Sunday Independent* that "Johnny Logan was a name from ancient history, a broken star touring the cabaret spots to bored audiences, singing a song that won the Eurovision, nobody was sure when."

Logan's had experienced a lot of personal suffering and unhappiness with his professional career.

Louis was the one person whose support for Logan was unending. He cared more about the singer as a friend than as a client. He was also one of the few people whose support and advice Logan valued. They both felt Logan's career was going nowhere. Louis, however, remained firm in the belief that Logan was a talented singer and songwriter and encouraged him to compete in the National Song Contest once more. Logan was wounded after his earlier setbacks but reluctantly agreed to try again, warning Louis that he would give up his singing and composing career if nothing came of it.

Maybe it was because of the adrenaline that last minute acts of desperation can sometimes engender, maybe it was luck, maybe it was just good timing, but in 1987 Johnny Logan wrote a great pop ballad called *Hold Me Now*. A few observers have suggested that it was Louis' utter belief in Logan's capabilities that spurred him to succeed. Logan performed the song himself at the National Song Contest held in the Gaiety Theatre on 8 March. He won. It was a triumphant success for Louis, who believed he had pulled Logan out of a deep career rut. For the third time, Louis and Logan were off to the Eurovision, this time in Brussels. Between the national finals and the Eurovision proper, Louis and Logan spoke every day on the phone. "Coming up to the show, he was on the phone to me night and day. He was working at it," recalls Louis.

The 1987 Contest threw up the usual number of bizarre entrants. There was Lotta Engberg, with her song *Fyra bugg och en coka cola*, which translated as *Four Gums and a Coca Cola*. While her song had sailed through the Swedish finals, there was outrage at such obvious product placement when she reached the Eurovision, and she had to change the song's title to *Boogaloo*. The Israeli entrants, Datner & Kushnir, also caused a bit of a stir with their song about homeless people in their native country. The song was called *Shir Habatlanim*, which translates as *The Bums*.

65

On arrival in Brussels, Logan was greeted as a superstar. Because he had won the Contest in 1980, he was recognised and applauded wherever he went. He was revered for his achievement of seven years previous, which Louis and Logan found uplifting. The singer was greeted with chants of "Johnny, Johnny, Johnny" on the streets. Unlike his previous experiences with the Eurovision, Louis felt confident. Admittedly, it is not always easy for a manager to be an objective judge of his own act, but he believed a win was possible. And he was right.

There was no close-run, edge-of-the-seat voting tension in the Palais de Centenaire, where the event was staged. Logan won with 172 points, one of the highest winning scores ever, and 31 points ahead of the German entry, *Wind*.

In the press conference following his win, Logan said his success was due to everyone who had stood by him since 1980. He was speaking about Louis Walsh.

"Louis was the one person who never lost faith in Johnny over the years," says Healy. "He kept the flag flying."

Louis genuinely felt for his friend. It is true that Louis is a businessman first and foremost, and realised the earning potential Logan had at that point, but he wanted Logan to succeed, as much out of friendship as anything else. He also believed Logan deserved credit for his achievements.

"It was fantastic because nobody had ever won it twice before. He wrote the song. It was his chance to make all the money and become famous again. He just lived, he lived every minute of it. He had fantastic self-belief and he proved everybody wrong and he won, and he had a huge hit record and made a lot of money that time around."

Louis saw the business opportunity straight away. No-one had ever won the Eurovision twice before. He had been pressing copies of Logan's single on anyone who would take it all week, but he decided to stop handing out promotional copies after the Contest, telling journalists and industry figures attending the after-show party to buy the record.

The win took the music industry in Ireland by surprise. Each of the major record shops had taken only the minimum order of *Hold Me Now*, which was 25 copies. The record company CBS, which had signed Logan for the second time, hurriedly organised the pressing of another quarter of a million copies of the single.

It is both an advantage and a disadvantage of celebrity that the general public tends to have a short memory. After his second win, the Irish public and media completely forgot how they had sniggered at Logan's earlier downfall and turned out in their thousands to welcome him home.

When his flight landed at Dublin Airport, Logan stared out of the window in disbelief at the five thousand fans waiting to greet him. He clutched at Healy for support saying "Oh God, I've waited for this." It was déja-vû for all concerned.

Once again, Logan had to brave the multitude of fans at the airport, but this time it was so much sweeter. Seven years of self-doubt vanished among the cries of "We love you, Johnny" and the banners declaring "We're holding you now". Louis, of course, was ecstatic and elated. He was the manager of this double Eurovision-winning wunderkind and he was making the most of it. "He is made for life," Louis declared rather grandly to the waiting media, "and this time he has control over his own affairs. The bookings are already flooding in. Nearly every European country wants him to do a TV show."

Logan immediately set off on another tour of European cities, appearing on TV shows, being interviewed by the newspapers, and enjoying the plaudits wherever he went. He even appeared on the Royal Variety Performance, exhorting the Queen to hold him now. The single went to No. 2 in the UK charts, and No. 1 in the Irish charts, and sold six million copies in total, twice as many as *What's Another Year* had sold. Logan was back, Louis was in charge, but then disaster struck.

Bewilderingly, Logan's career crashed and burned for the second time in seven years. There was no fracas between sparring managers. There was only one record company involved. The ingredients for lasting success were there, but the momentum wasn't. His career simply fizzled out. He was good-looking, he could sing, and he had a certain song-writing talent. What on earth went wrong?

Eurovision expert Geoff Harrison believes there were two main reasons for Logan's second fall from grace. "In 1987, when Johnny Logan won the Eurovision Song Contest, it wasn't as popular as it is now," he says. "It was quite popular in the late sixties and the early seventies, and then it sort of faded round about 1975 or 1976 and really didn't make it back into popularity until some time in the mid-nineties, until all those Irish wins. That really boosted its popularity. I think he hit it at a time when it wasn't really that big a thing to be the winner of the Eurovision Song Contest."

Bad timing wasn't the only problem, according to Harrison: "I think he also had a style that didn't really fit in at the time. The style, while it was a winning style for the Song Contest, was not necessarily a winning style with the public. I think there's a market that likes this sort of stuff but won't buy it. It's the Radio 2 market in Britain. You listen to it and you never buy it."

Another major problem was the divergent views held by Logan and Louis on what direction the singer's career should take. Louis wanted Logan to target the middle of the road market. Logan, however, sought musical credibility and saw himself as more of a rock star.

"I would have liked him to be middle of the road," says Louis. "All these young guys, they want to be hip and trendy. They don't want to be safe. They don't want to be middle of the road. If you're middle of the road, you'll never get knocked down. I just thought he was famous, he did well, but he could have been global. But who was to know? He didn't know. I didn't know. Nobody knew around that time.

"We can all look back and say, 'If only we had done this'. He has still done very well. I just think he could have been great, because I do think he had the talent and the looks, and he worked very hard. I think he had too many chiefs and not enough Indians. That's being really honest.

"If I was managing him now, I'd get him American producers. I wouldn't go with the producers we were using at the time."

The rock journalist George Byrne, who knew all parties involved, says Logan should have listened more to Louis.

"Logan's idea of a rock star wouldn't be anyone else's idea of a rock star. Louis saw what was going on. He was right. He tried to pitch him as a Cliff Richard type with longevity, doing middle of the road stuff and working forever. Logan wanted to be more like Sting or Robert Palmer. It was an essential clash and it was never going to happen."

While Logan must shoulder some of the blame for his career falling apart, so must Louis. The two parted on good terms and remain friends. But if Louis been a truly effective and professional manager in 1987, he could possibly have tried harder to persuade Logan away from his rock leanings for a while. After all, in later years he talked his acts into doing whatever was necessary to keep the hits rolling in.

While Logan never cracked the UK market, he has enjoyed success in Scandinavia, and like the BayWatch actor, David Hasselhoff, he made it big in Germany. He is signed to Sony in Denmark and his last album even went gold there. Sales like these mean that Logan can tour, earning himself a comfortable living. Had Louis been as powerful or experienced in 1987 as he is now, there is little doubt that Johnny Logan would still be signed to Sony in London, rather than Sony in Copenhagen.

The collapse of Logan's career in Ireland hit Louis hard. It had been his one chance to escape the grind of life as just another agent back in Dublin. That chance vanished overnight and Louis' confidence was badly dented.

Although Logan's career floundered, both he and Louis had the consolation of knowing that he was one of the Eurovision greats. "If anyone starts to think of Eurovision stars," explains Geoff Harrison, "they think generally of ABBA, and then Johnny Logan. And then, if they get desperate, they remember that Celine Dion won it once, and if somebody asks me, I'll say Julio Eglesias was in it once, but he tries to forget it. But Johnny Logan really is up there. Nobody did what

Johnny Logan did. He's Mr. Eurovision. There's a few that have entered more than once but nobody's ever won more than one. That's what makes him special. He's a classic."

5

WHY ME?

In December 1989, Carol Hanna decided to leave Hayden's company. It was not an acrimonious split. Hanna just wanted to have her own business. She set up Carol and Associates at 90 Lower Baggot Street and became an agent for various acts with whom she already worked closely. Although she broke from Tommy Hayden Enterprises on friendly terms, setting up on her own was daunting. She had worked alongside Louis and Hayden for 20 years.

"I had been with Tommy for twenty-odd years at that stage," says Hanna. "I had been with him a long time and the break was very, very difficult."

Initially, Louis decided to remain with Hayden's firm but when Hanna left, it was just a matter of time before he followed. Four months later, he went to work at 90 Lower Baggot Street. Hayden, who had been like a father to him, wished him all the best. "It was a good little partnership. It worked out well. And we made a few bob in the meantime, and we always paid our bills."

"Tommy Hayden was very honest," says Louis. "He didn't shaft anyone at all. He was a nice man and he wasn't ruthless. If he were more ruthless, he probably would have been more successful. I learned a lot. And he was also good at hyping records, trying to get airplay. He was very good at all that. I did learn a lot from him in that respect."

"Myself and Carol wanted to stay in the live music thing, because we didn't know anything else. We worked there for ages just selling bands, selling anything we could, be it a DJ, be it a band. I used to bring in acts from England like Sinitta, Sonia, Bronski Beat, Hazel O'Connor. I would buy them for eggs, and sell them for wine, and try and make money around the country."

Although the two were effectively sole traders operating from the same office, many people in the music industry came to believe one was in charge of the other.

"People always thought I worked for him all the way through," says Hanna. "We worked together. We managed Linda Martin together and Who's Eddie and we had our own individual businesses then. He had his own thing with bands but we always worked together, and I always looked after everything for him. I always did everything, office work and things like that. I was doing it for myself so I would do it for him as well."

The business was harder than expected. Their respective fledgling businesses found it hard to make ends meet. The two found it difficult to keep the office in Baggot Street. The cost of renting was prohibitive, prompting Hanna to begin working at home.

"I made an office in one of the rooms in my house and set it up there, so Louis said to me 'Well, what'll I do?' So I said, 'Come with me' and he did."

Although Louis was his own boss by this stage, the years after leaving Tommy Hayden were some of the worst of his career. The local music industry was as ruthless as it ever was and Louis still had to deal with the sharks of the business.

"The worst thing was not getting paid. Promoters just did not care," he recalls. "It was a Catch 22 situation. We needed them and we couldn't pull out because we needed them for someone else the following week. You just wouldn't get paid. They were in control and they didn't care. They were the most awful people. That's why today, I've got agents, really top agents, and I do not begrudge them for making the money at all."

Rock music continued to dominate the scene in Ireland in the late 1980s and early 1990s. Although Louis didn't personally like the music, or the lifestyle that went with it, his job was to secure concerts and arrange tours for emerging Irish rock talent. He describes this period as "soul destroying".

"I didn't like their music and I didn't like their attitude. They had all these tour managers, roadies and gofers running around the country," he says.

The emerging talent he worked with included Aslan, Light A Big Fire, No Sweat, Paul Cleary and the Partisans, Fountainhead, Power of Dreams and In Tua Nua.

"Some of the more talented ones were great but some of the others had dreadful wanker managers," he says. "I would book out tours and I would be on 10 percent. And they wouldn't pay me at the end of the tour. That happened me with this horrible manager who managed [names band]. He was really, really awful. There were other managers who were really difficult."

Of all the rock bands that sought his services, he believes Cry Before Dawn had the most potential.

"I liked them a lot. They were one of the best bands. And I thought they could have gone a lot more. I thought Brendan Wade was a real talent. There was so much talent around the country, but they didn't get any record deals. It was all about getting record deals and that was the most important thing. You were at the mercy of A&R people in London, who just came over here and signed everything that moved because it was Irish; they were looking for the next U2," he adds.

Louis found working with rock bands tedious, tiresome and frustrating. At times he wondered if he would have better off to take a steady nine to five job. As it was, he ran into financial difficulties on a monthly basis.

"He went through dodgy periods, where as far as I know his rent was in jeopardy," recalls Tommy Hayden.

Carol Hanna, who was by far Louis' closest ally both professionally and personally, helped him any way she could.

"When Louis was financially very, very low, he was my friend, and I looked after everything for him, and that was it," she says.

He persevered with the business, organising concerts in small venues like the Rock Garden in Dublin's Temple Bar and the Baggot Inn on Dublin's southside.

"I had bands playing in every toilet in the country, I worked all the college circuit as well. It was very hard to make money. By the time you paid for your office and overheads, you had nothing left."

He acknowledges that life on the gig circuit was also difficult for the artists he booked out. "Especially the girls, because there were no dressing rooms," he says. "I used to hate going to the gigs with them because they were treated so badly. You really were treated as if you were a second-class citizen.

"You would never, ever know with some promoters in Ireland because they would always have back doors. They were never honest. They never paid what they were supposed to pay and that's why they made all the money."

The media gave him equally short shrift. He couldn't develop any reliable newspaper or television connections. No one would take his calls; messages went unanswered and the national broadcaster, in particular, would ignore him.

"The media was totally sown up by people in RTE. You know, you'd never get on RTE. The *Late Late Show* wouldn't even take your phone calls. The media generally think 'Oh, Irish bands, they're only Irish bands, they don't matter'."

Louis' confidence was at an all-time low during this time. He considered giving up on more than one occasion, disillusioned by the reality of a career in Irish showbusiness. With the exception of a few close friends, he had a keen distrust of everyone else in the business. He saw his adversaries constantly putting him down and treating him poorly. In time, he learned to ignore them and trust his own instincts.

"It was hard but a valuable learning experience. You have to believe in yourself and you just have to keep going. You can't listen to other people like Irish promoters. If I had listened to them, I would still be booking bands out in pubs and they would think they were doing me the favour, giving me the gig for £600.

"I used to book out Brush Shiels and acts like that. That was soul-destroying, going into Bad Bobs and then see all these drunk people dancing to the Fields of Athenry and Thin Lizzy again, the same old stuff," he says, quickly adding that "Brush was great."

"But I used to hate the Irish culture, getting drunk, singing diddly-aye songs and then going home and fighting. I wasn't into it. There was no entertainment in it for me at all. It was just a job.

"I didn't know anything else and I didn't want to work in a nine-to-five job. I would hate a normal routine. I don't like any kind of normality. People in boxes, doing routine nine-to-five and going to Mass on Sundays and going to Croke Park. I hate all that thing with Irish people. I do not like the routine they have. I have to be myself and do what I like. I always have been like that. I've always done what I wanted to do."

When Louis stopped managing Johnny Logan, the two had agreed to regroup if the opportunity arose. No one thought Logan would ever consider participating again in the Eurovision, which had caused him so much grief in the past. Though he was scorched by the Eurovision experience, he still had a deep desire to succeed. The attraction of fame and popular acclaim proved a strong incentive. In 1992, when Louis approached Logan once more and urged him to write a song for Linda Martin, he agreed.

"To win the Eurovision Song Contest was a big thing. You were literally catapulted into superstardom all over Europe," explains Linda Martin.

"I'm not a singer/songwriter, so we reckoned we would clinch a very lucrative career if we could win the Eurovision. So Louis went off and did what he usually does, looking for songs and writers and all sorts of things. Johnny Logan had been a pal of ours for many years. Johnny had came up the song in 1984 and we came second that year. So we thought, 'that was close, let's go again'."

Logan wrote a song called *Why Me?* for Martin to perform. If nothing else, he had extensive experience of the Eurovision and he was satisfied that *Why Me?* was a possible contender for the National Song Contest.

It was Martin's ninth time entering the Contest. Since 1984, she had entered on another two occasions, in 1989; when she came sixth and in 1990; when she came second. Her luck had to change eventually. In 1992, Martin won the Irish Contest.

"It's called perseverance," says Louis of the effort. "It's called trying, trying, trying. I thought Chips were perfect for the Eurovision. The boys and the girls, like Brotherhood of Man or Bucks Fizz. I thought they were great, but the Irish public always voted for the wrong song. She wanted it so badly. But *Why Me?* was the perfect ballad. We were out to win, totally, totally."

The 1992 Contest was held in the Swedish city of Malmo. Competition was quite stiff that year, particularly as the UK had sent musical heavyweight Michael Ball, who was at the peak of his fame as a singer. Ball had fame on his side, but Martin gave a better performance on the night. She won the Eurovision with 155 points to Ball's 137. It wasn't just a Eurovision win, it was vindication for her, for Logan, and for Louis; that they had been right to persevere with the Eurovision.

The night was even more special for Louis, as he had always stood by Martin and she was one of the few close friends he had in the music business. The 1992 contest also marked a landmark for Johnny Logan. With his ambition of a third win fulfilled, he finally stepped away from the Eurovision. "I will never take part in the Eurovision again. This is the last time you will see me here," he vowed to reporters. True to his word, he never did enter another song into the Contest.

Martin arrived home in Ireland to acclaim but not to adulation. Her Eurovision win was overshadowed by far bigger news. On the same weekend, Bishop Eamonn Casey, one of the better known and most outspoken members of the Irish clergy, had admitted that he had a lengthy relationship with a woman named Annie Murphy, fathered her son, and "borrowed" £70,000 from diocesan funds to make maintenance payments. Ireland was gripped by the story, the first of many scandals to rock the Irish Catholic Church. Page after page of the newspapers and hour after hour of air-time was devoted to the subject, leaving little media space for Louis to exploit.

"At that stage the Eurovision had sort of plummeted and, although certainly career-wise it was a wonderful thing that happened and I still live off it to a certain extent, it just wasn't the monumental thing that it was in years gone by," says Martin.

"We kind of knew that the Eurovision wasn't as big as it was but it was still guaranteed to work and guaranteed to raise your profile," adds Louis. "You got a record deal and you could work with some people. She got some TV out of it. She got her own show. RTE gave her some work. I know her very well and I like her. She likes what she does and that's the good thing about her. She is passionate about it."

Neither she nor Louis were under any illusions that she would be performing on *Top of the Pops*. Louis had finally realised that the Eurovision was not the best way to create an international pop star. When Logan won the Contest a second time but still failed to make it, Louis realised that the Eurovision did not give an artist or an artist's manager a guaranteed career in the UK and Ireland.

Eurovision winners are, however, always sure to secure lucrative work in Europe, where the markets are more receptive to their style of singing. Eurovision expert Geoff Harrison explains: "The record market in Germany is at least as big as the British one and it's a real market. We tend to think of these songs only in terms of our own market. Britain still likes to think of itself in terms of leading the world in popular music, which I think it doesn't any more. It certainly has a hand in it, but American pop music is certainly bigger, and there's a lot of European stuff around. I think it comes with a rather curious attitude of 'Those Europeans, they're nothing to do with us'. It's part of the British anti-European attitude, that Europe is somewhere else."

While Louis' involvement over the years in Eurovision has meant a lot to him as a huge fan of the Contest, it was also important in another way. For a few weeks here and there, it lifted him out of the drudgery of booking gigs for ungrateful bands at home, and showed him that there was more to managing artists.

Niall Stokes, editor of *Hot Press*, elaborates: "He got involved with people who had higher aspirations, in a way, certainly in terms of wanting to be internationally successful, when he worked with various Eurovision outfits. He got a flavour of what it was like dealing in the international arena when he was working with those people. He'd have been at least peripherally involved in negotiations with international record companies or management companies and probably more directly with the guys who were putting tours together for the likes of Johnny Logan and Linda Martin internationally. I suppose at that stage he figured it was something he could do as well as any of the other guys who were out there doing it – and what has happened subsequently certainly bears that assumption out."

By the early 1990s, Louis knew there was a chance he could cut it as a manager in the cut throat business of pop music. He had already come so close. He had the drive and the commitment to make it work. All he needed now was a good idea.

6

BOYZONE

"**L**ouis would appear in your office because he knew everybody, he didn't need an appointment, he just arrived. He was sitting there one day and he said 'I've got this great idea. I have two journalists on board already'."

Although Paul Keogh is speaking on the telephone, you can sense that he is smiling as he remembers Louis announcing his "great idea".

It was late 1993 and the managing director of Polygram Ireland was as amused as everyone else in the music industry when Louis declared he was forming a new Irish boyband to compete directly with Take That.

"Everybody knew him at that stage. He wasn't that successful. He was the guy going around bitching about rock bands. That's how most people would remember him, giving out about Hothouse Flowers."

Louis was sneered at when he first came up with the idea. It's not hard to see why. He was a struggling agent, who had managed a few Eurovision acts, and who had failed to make any serious money after more than twenty years in the business. He admits himself he was penniless in 1993. He was perceived as soft, too soft to successfully create and manage a boyband.

There were other hurdles for him to overcome. Ireland was known for producing some of the best creative and successful rock acts in the world. Ireland didn't produce pop boybands. But Louis was entranced by the idea and was openly passionate about taking on Take That.

Working in his favour was a huge network of media contacts. Had he not been broke, and had he not cultivated influential journalists as friends, Boyzone might never have happened.

He came up with the idea after watching a concert by East 17 staged at the Point Theatre in Dublin, and had come away unimpressed, and surprised that such a major pop act mimed so much. Shortly afterwards, he went to see Take That, also at the Point.

"I thought Take That were absolutely great," says Louis. "It was a great show and I liked Gary Barlow. He was the star for me, and if I had been offered Gary or Robbie, I would have taken Gary, because I thought the guy was brilliant. I was a fan of his and I thought they put on an amazing show. I was really excited that night at the Point."

After thinking about the concert and listening to their records, he came to the conclusion that boybands were more an overall entertainment package than a collection of singers. He was inspired by the notion of creating a band made up of distinct characters, each of whom would appeal to a different audience, and not all of whom had to be strong singers. He began to mull over the possibility of setting up an Irish boyband. The idea became a preoccupation, and soon began to consume all his energy. He was determined to assess the viability of his idea.

By his own admission, he was afraid of defeat. "Things were not good for me at the time," he says. "I remember telling these journalists I was thinking of doing a boyband. I was very unsure about it. I was very afraid of it. I didn't want to fall and I didn't have any money. The journalists wrote about it and my phone started ringing and that was it. I couldn't turn back."

In November 1993, Louis' friends in the newspapers wrote stories flagging the auditions. The free publicity worked. Over 300 young men arrived for the open aud-itions for Louis' boyband. The auditions were held at the Ormond Centre, a giant warehouse situated on Dublin's Ormond Quay, overlooking the river Liffey. Among those who turned up to try out for the new band were singers, dancers, musicians and actors.

The auditions were time-consuming and most of those who turned up did not have the necessary looks or talent. Louis asked each auditionee to sing a song and dance to the Right Said Fred song *I'm Too Sexy*. Louis weeded out about 50 who were passable and asked them to come back a week later.

"Ronan came in, Stephen came in. I knew Ronan had something. He just sold himself to me almost imme-diately. He was chirpy, happy and he looked the part. He was all eager beaver. So I knew we had him. He sang *Father and Son* at the auditions.

"Stephen was ringing me all the time wanting to be in the band. He was really keen. He sent me a brilliant CV, brilliant pictures of himself. And he was just great on the night, really chirpy. We basically put the band around them."

After another round of singing and dancing, he compiled a short-list of 10 and invited them to audition for a third and final time. Of the 10, he chose six: Keith Duffy, Stephen Gately, Ronan Keating, Shane Lynch, Richard Rock, and Mark Walton. Louis had found the boys, but now he had to make them into a band. Before embarking on this project, he decided to ride out the mini-wave of publicity the auditions had generated and wangled the act a spot on the *Late Late Show*, Ireland's most watched programme.

"They were on the *Late Late Show* that Friday, which was a real chance. Who else would have got that chance? So they were in studio, dancing, making pricks of themselves to the Irish public, which everybody laughs at now, but at least they were on the TV," he adds.

Those five minutes on air have haunted Boyzone ever since. The band hadn't rehearsed, and had no songs prepared. Instead, they danced to a backing track. What started off as a loose routine degenerated into random lunging and gyrating. Shane Lynch grabbed his crotch repeatedly. Stephen Gately appeared to be limboing under an invisible bar. Ronan Keating grinned maniacally. Keith Duffy showed off an oiled torso clad in nothing more than a pair of red braces. They were breathtakingly awful.

The show's host Gay Byrne thanked Boyzone for their "act" and wished them well, quite clearly believing he would never see or hear of them again.

Louis believed the benefits of the publicity far outweighed the embarrassment. People were now talking about Boyzone. To their credit, most of the band's members had some stage experience. Stephen Gately had five years worth of vocal and dance training, and had done some acting and modelling. Ronan Keating had been in a band called Nameste, which won the £1000 first prize in a local talent competition. Keith Duffy had played drums in two bands, and had worked as a strippogram. Mikey Graham, who joined the group belatedly, had gone to singing, dancing and acting classes as a child, and had aspirations of becoming a songwriter.

Graham's induction into Boyzone was precipitated by the loss of two of its original members, Richie Rock and Mark Walton. Rock, the son of showband singer Dickie Rock, was asked to leave after just two months.

Mark Walton also left at the same time. "Mark Walton and Richard Rock we had to drop. Mark Walton, because he didn't fit in. He was a nice guy. The reason I put Richard in the band is because I thought Dickie was a household name, a man that came from nothing and made an awful lot of himself," says Louis.

"Dickie came and talked to me twice about it, asking me to give Richard another chance. I think Dickie is a great man, but his son at the time, just didn't fit in."

Louis believed it was imperative that the band worked well together and had no compunction in asking the two boys to leave.

"The problem is, the other four are going to suffer. It's their careers. You only get one chance at this. It's like having a football team. If somebody is not right, they're going to contaminate it. It's like having a bad apple in a box of apples. You have to get rid of it. We had to do that. You're only as good as your weakest link."

Mickey Graham, having been the "best of the rest" at the auditions, was chosen as the replacement member. At 20 years of age, he was the oldest of the band members. Keith Duffy was 18, both Shane Lynch and Stephen Gately were 17, and Ronan Keating was only 16.

In the beginning, the group was not particularly dedicated to their new career as pop stars. Louis frequently left them to their own devices. Sometimes, they'd rehearse for 20 minutes and head straight to the pub.

Louis was busy elsewhere, trying to get Boyzone off the ground. He had arranged a photo session with a photographer and was touting the resulting photographs around to everyone he could think of in the music industry. Behind his back he was being ridiculed.

"Everyone was laughing at me. There were all these trendy rock managers. They were all falling around laughing at me, I remember distinctly, as were people at the record companies, saying 'here he goes again'. They didn't see the market," says Louis.

One of those to show an interest, having seen the photographs was Tom Watkins, at the time manager of East 17, and an influential figure in the UK music industry.

Watkins met Louis and the band in the Shelbourne Hotel in Dublin for tentative talks about getting involved.

"I went over and saw him and the boys and I thought they were all right. It's difficult to get a bunch together. I don't think Ronan necessarily shone at that particular moment, apart from that Louis knew he had a great voice."

Although Watkins recognised that Boyzone could have a future, he did not get involved.

"I'd done Bros, I'd done East 17," he says. "I really didn't want to get involved in another boyband unless they paid me a fortune. There would have to be some kind of incentive to want to do it and I said to Louis, 'Well, if you pay me this, I'll do it', and it was just a way of saying No, in a kind way. I went onto to give them all sorts of support spots when they were launching their career and Louis and I would continue on the phone nattering about tactics and politics, and structure, and manipulating record companies. I think that there was no arrogance on my part not to get involved, but I had just tired of that whole boyband thing."

Louis recalls a different story. "He (Watkins) wanted to do a deal. He wanted to control the whole thing but I wouldn't let him," says Louis.

Boyzone were not to have the heavyweight backing of Watkins but Louis persisted with other leads and persuaded Paul Keogh of Polygram to sign a three single distribution deal.

Louis has said it was extremely difficult to get any record label to Boyzone but Keogh insists it wasn't like that. "That's a myth, that Louis had to work really hard to get the record company to sign them. I put up quarter of a million pounds very quickly, so there was no struggle from Louis' point of view." Keogh has since left the music industry and runs the international marketing division of JCB in the UK.

"Keogh basically signed the band because he liked the look and he took a chance," says Louis. "He was one of those guys who would take a chance. He was one of the few Irish record company guys that wanted to be successful, didn't just want to keep the local stuff on the shelves. Most of the other majors are just warehouse managers. They almost don't want to have a local act because then they have to work it. It means their bosses in England are watching them.

"He took a chance. Mind you, we did pay for the recording of the record. But he did package it very well because he was quite a good marketing guy. He had come from Budweiser. He liked the pictures and he took a chance and he said it would be a bit fun," says Louis.

Now he had a distribution deal but he had to find a suitable song, and a producer willing to record it. Ever a fan of pop hits from the past, he decided Boyzone should record a cover version of the Detroit Spinners' song *Working My Way Back To You*. This was the song that had knocked Johnny Logan from the No. 1 spot in Ireland back in 1980, which was possibly why it had stuck in Louis' mind.

Few in the music industry took him seriously. Producers, in particular, ignored his calls seeking help.

"I was ringing promoters and record companies. Simon Cowell wouldn't take my calls. I was ringing every first, second, third-rate producer. Nobody would talk to me. I couldn't get anybody. I had no money. All I had was an office," Louis recalls.

The uncertainty he faced became even more disquieting in those weeks. Word quickly spread that Louis was desperate. From then on, the industry was even more reluctant to entertain him. So far, he had failed to make any impact at all. In his calmer moments, he would talk to a few close friends and anxiously recount the tribulations he was facing. It was an unnerving time where his confidence was tested.

He was still determined and kept calling any contact willing to take his telephone calls. He was terror stricken at the thoughts of failing. Eventually, he was directed to a producer called Ian Levine at the Tropicana recording studio in London. Levine agreed to cut the record.

This was great news but there was a snag. The recording would cost £10,000, which Louis, who was virtually penniless, didn't have. Louis did not know what to do next. He turned to John Reynolds, the owner of the POD nightclub in Dublin, who he had known for about ten years. Reynolds used to work for his father who owned a ballroom in Co. Longford.

"I used to book Louis' bands over the phone but I actually never met him," says Reynolds. "I didn't meet him for about six years. Then, when I was in college in Dublin, I used to call into his office almost every evening on my way home. I used to learn more in his office than I did all day in Trinity College."

By early 1994, Louis and Reynolds were good friends. The two were part of a close-knit circle, who confided and trusted in one another. Reynolds remembers that Louis had talked at length about his idea for the previous six months.

"I actually, in a very strange way, thought he would do it," says Reynolds.

"One day I was in Café Java on Leeson St. with my then-girlfriend, and Louis rang me and said 'Where are you? Café Java? I'm going to come down to you and ask you something.' So, he came down and he said, 'You know, we've done the auditions and the guys were on the *Late Late Show*, but we can't get a record deal. Do you want to be involved?' And I said, 'Yeah, I'd love to'.

"He said, 'John, I'll take care of all the music and you take care of the business stuff, and we're going to need money to shoot a video and record a video.' That's basically how it started. There wasn't any highfalutin negotiation. I think it lasted maybe ten minutes. The following Friday, Ronan picked up money from me and they recorded the first single in the UK and the rest, as they say, is history."

The deal was straightforward. For his initial investment, Reynolds would receive half of any management commission earned by Boyzone. Although

Reynolds realised he had everything to lose, he consoled himself with the thought that he could also have everything to gain. Louis had his full confidence.

Louis and Boyzone travelled to London to record their first single. Louis was jubilant because he was finally on his way to London to cut a single. But his mood changed when he arrived.

"Levine told me the boys couldn't sing," says Louis. "We all went over and I remember the boys had never been in London before. Most of them had never been in studios before, and most of them haven't been in studios since either!

"I wanted this Detroit Spinners record *Working My Way Back To You* because I thought it was a great fun record. So Ian Levine had the backing track made before we went over. We had to pay him the £10,000 in advance."

Louis was still unsure of his product and Levine's remarks didn't help. The producer wasn't acting out of malice or stupidity, but he left an indelible impression on the teenagers, who burned with rage at his remarks about their singing capabilities.

"We recorded the song," says Louis. "But it just didn't suit the boys, the way he had recorded it; it was too high. So he put Mikey Graham and Stephen singing on it, and he called me out of the studio and said 'The little blonde fella can't sing.' That was Ronan."

Louis stood motionless, not really knowing what to do. Driven by his commitment to make his idea work, he took the producer's advice. He dropped Keating; Gately and Graham sang instead. It was not an easy decision to make because Louis already admired Keating and had faith in his talent.

"He [Levine] was somebody I looked up to because he had made some great disco tracks before. It was a bad start for me in England," recalls Louis.

One episode in London helped to restore the band's shaken confidence. "We went into this local restaurant somewhere in London, and the girl in the restaurant said 'Oh, are ye the new Take That?' So we kind of knew they had something going for them," says Louis. The waitresses throwaway comment was a fine piece of good fortune. It was exactly what the teenagers needed to hear.

Even at 16, Ronan Keating had an unbreakable self-belief, which some observers could have mistaken for arrogance. He persuaded Louis to let him record another song, the B-side to the single. They chose the Cat Stevens song *Father and Son*, Keating's party piece and a song he'd performed at the Boyzone auditions. Louis agreed and paid £600 to record it in the STS recording studio in Dublin. The band then made a video for the single. The video cost £4000 to make and looked every penny of it.

Despite the amateurish feel to the whole enterprise, the song quickly rose to No. 3 in the charts when it was released in Ireland in March 1994.

"Riverdance was really hot at the time and Wet Wet Wet had *Love is All Around* so our record only went to No. 3 but it was fantastic at the time," says Louis. "We did our first PA down in HMV in Henry St. There was like a thousand kids and that's when it all started. It was absolutely huge in Dublin. When we went down the country, there would be 100 or 150 people there some nights. It was great training for the boys. They got paid £60 a night each for the gigs. That got them ready for the big time, I suppose."

The music critics howled in derision, particularly as the song hadn't merited a UK release, but Louis didn't care. He was vindicated. The band had a top three hit in Ireland and they were on their way.

7

FROM BOYZ TO MEN

In the early days of Boyzone, the group trusted Louis implicitly. Whatever he said went. The band had complete faith in him. They trusted him emphatically and never doubted his judgment. It really was necessary for Louis to push Boyzone as hard as possible. He believed the best way to break the band and recoup the time and money invested in it was to tour Ireland extensively.

Touring would serve to raise Boyzone's profile and, just as importantly, to teach the fledgling pop stars that succeeding in showbusiness is hard work.

He told them in no uncertain terms that they had to go out and work. He wanted them to play in any venue that would accommodate a crowd, no matter how small. He used his contacts across Ireland to secure gigs for Boyzone and sent the group off in a white transit van.

"It was hard work but I was loving it," says Keating. "I was happy to be doing something and I loved music. I was just glad to be getting up on stage every night and singing. We got a couple of quid into our pocket, more money than I was earning. It was some of the best years in the band for me. It was fantastic. It was brilliant."

Boyzone worked harder than they ever imagined they could. They played everywhere. They would perform *Working My Way Back To You* at least twice every night, sometimes more, because their repertoire was so limited. They played in innumerable venues – village halls, pubs, and nightclubs, where they would come on in the middle of the disco. They played at the annual Rose of Tralee festival. For most of the gigs, the band members earned £60.

Although his detractors found Louis' latest venture laughable, he persevered. He often accompanied the band on their travels, not just to ensure that they were working as hard as he wanted them to, but to support them and buoy their spirits.

"I'll always remember Louis sitting in the back of the white transit van with the five of us, and I remember that people would be calling him on the phone; journalists and famous people. We'd be amazed at his mobile phone ringing and all these people calling him," says Keating.

"I've always had this image of him sitting in the corner of the van. We used to come back at 2 a.m. or 3 a.m. in the morning, freezing cold in the back of this van and Louis with a kind of an old blanket over his head and he looked like Peig Sayers. It was hilarious."

The singer has fond memories of the time, which he describes in his autobiography as some of the best of his life. "We were drinking cans in the back of the van, returning home early in the morning; the other lads had parked their cars outside my house. Then we'd meet at the Royal Dublin Hotel in O'Connell Street the next day after work and off we'd go again to another gig, maybe in Galway, or Cork or Donegal. We did it because we loved it."

Louis Walsh (to the right) aged 10. He attended Kiltimagh Boys National School before attending St. Nathy's boarding school. As a child, he detested working on his father's farm.

Left: Louis with his older sister, Evelyn, to whom he is very close. When Louis moved to Dublin, he stayed in Evelyn's apartment. As children, they used to dance to their father's records.

Below: The Walsh family home on Chapel Street, Kiltimagh.

Facing page: Louis with Carol Hanna in Tommy Hayden's office. The agent was instrumental in guiding Louis through his teengage years. "Louis and myself bounded from the start. We were like brother and sister."

Previous pages: Johnny Logan. Louis met Logan on a bus and offered to manage him on the spot.
© Photocall Ireland/Gareth Chaney

Linda Martin. She won the Eurovision after entering it for the ninth time. Louis describes her effort as sheer perseverance.
© Photocall Ireland/Eamonn Farrell

Above: Boyzone. Clockwise from left: Stephen Gately, Keith Duffy, Shane Lynch, Mikey Graham and Ronan Keating in Dublin Airport after arriving from London to celebrate the success of their single "Key to my life" going straight to No. 1 in the Irish charts.
© Photocall Ireland/Leon Farrell

Facing page, above: John Reynolds at the opening of U2's nightclub, The Kitchen. Reynold's is a trusted confidante of Louis Walsh's.
© Photocall Ireland/Eamonn Farrell

Facing page, below: Paul Keogh with the singer, Kerri-Ann. Louis and Boyzone referred to Keogh as 'God'.
© Photocall Ireland/Leon Farrell

Facing page: Louis celebrates Boyzone's success in the Chocolate Bar, owned by John Reynolds.
© Irish Examiner

Above: Louis with his mother, Maureen. She remains the most influential person in his life.

Below: Frank and Maureen Walsh. Louis had a close relationship with his father.

Above: Louis with his six brothers: Paul, Frank, Eamonn, Padraig, Joseph and Noel

Below: The Walsh family home on Chapel Street as it looks now.

Facing page: Louis at the wedding of Bryan McFadden, a member of Westlife.
© Photocall Ireland/Cathy Loughran

Above: Bellefire: From left: Cathy Newell, Kelly Kilfeather, Ciara Newell an
Tara Lee.
© Sean Dwyer

Below: Westlife: At a time when the world seemed to have enough
boybands, Louis created Westlife. The band released a string of singles tha
reached No. 1. From left: Mark Feehily, Kian Egan, Shane Filan, Nicky Byrr
and Bryan McFadden.
© Photocall Ireland / Graham Hughes

Previous page: Samanth Mumba: Louis said Mumba instantly impressed him, that she reminded him of a young Janet Jackson or Toni Braxton.
© Sean Dwyer

Above: Omero Mumba at the Irish launch of Time Machine.
© Sean Dwyer

Facing page: Six on stage. From right: Sarah Keating, Kyle Anderson, Andy Orr, Emma O'Driscoll and Sinead Sheppard.
© Irish Examiner

Next page: Louis. "Unquestionably, Louis' greatest strength is that he can hear a song and know if that song can be a hit," John Reynolds said.

© Photocall Ireland / Kate Horgan

Boyzone travelled to virtually every provincial town in Ireland. On one occasion, they even played in Kiltimagh.

"I'll never forget going down to Kiltimagh for the first time," recalls Keating. "We all went down when we were on the Boyzone tour, the five of us. We went to Kiltimagh and we went to Louis' house. His Mam made us tea and we all sat around. We were all wrecked and we slept in the beds in the house. His Mam let us sleep in the beds. Louis arrived down a few hours later and he just couldn't deal with it. It was hilarious.

"Louis always built this wall around him, and we never really got to see the emotional side of Louis, or his family life. It was always Louis the businessman, our manager, to us. When we actually got to meet his family, we got to see another side of Louis, his mother giving out to him and saying 'Sit down there. Shut up. Eat your dinner'."

Incidentally, Louis' brother Frank says their mother was also given credit locally for her role in the success of Boyzone.

"When Boyzone were at their peak, she was walking down Castlebar, which would be the nearest kind of biggish town to us and somebody pointed to her and said 'There's the mother of Boyzone'."

As hard as Boyzone worked, Louis worked harder. He spent endless hours trying to secure media coverage in pop magazines. He also took care of the early marketing, which was aimed at young girls and women. At Boyzone's gigs, the female half of the audience usually reacted enthusiastically, although the men weren't always so welcoming. Bottles and cans of beer, coins, and lit cigarettes were often flung at the band.

Furthermore, Louis often found it difficult to extract an agreed fee from promoters, particularly if he personally wasn't there and Keating was left to collect the money owed to the band.

Although Boyzone had limited musical talent, the members of the group showed themselves to be completely dedicated to achieving success. This prompted Paul Keogh of Polygram Records to offer them an album deal.

Louis maintains he persuaded Keogh to make the deal, but Keogh himself says he offered it because the record company had already spent so much money on Boyzone. He says they needed to improve their chances of recouping it. With an album deal signed, Louis came up with the idea of recording *Love Me for a Reason*, an Osmonds song.

"Unquestionably Louis' greatest strength is that he can hear a song and know if that song would be a hit. He can hear a cover version and know what artist of his could sing it best," says Reynolds.

"Louis is notorious for staying up all night listening to music and I remember once he rang me in the middle of the night and said 'I've got the song for Boyzone. I've got the one that's going to be a smash hit' and I was like 'Yeah?' I was half asleep! I was like 'That's wonderful, Louis. Can I ring you in the morning?' He said, 'I'll play it to you. I'll play it to you' and it was *Love Me For A Reason* and I have to be honest, I wasn't convinced."

Reynolds says Louis became far more confident as the weeks passed by. In the early stages, he had not been aware of his own importance in the Irish music industry until Polygram offered Boyzone an album deal. A short while later, he was dictating the types of songs Boyzone should record, despite objections from the company.

"I was in a record company at the time when they slagged it off," recalls Reynolds. "But Louis kept saying, 'This is going to be a smash hit. This is going to break the band in England.' I have to say that I don't know anybody else close to it that had that belief in it. We were all taken along with this, including the record company in the UK and everywhere.

"I know that they were not sure about the record and it became a massive record. *Love Me For A Reason* in my view, was the song that not only broke Boyzone, but actually broke Louis."

Having chosen a song, Louis sought the services of well-known British producer Ray Hedges, who had often worked with Take That and was experienced in producing for the pop market.

"I got a phone call and someone said 'I've got another boy act for you'. I thought 'Oh no, what could this be?' you know, because I got sent a lot of projects after Take That. Some were really, really naff, but this guy was so full of enthusiasm," says Hedges of Louis.

"His enthusiasm won me over and I said 'What's the name?' and he said 'Boyzone', and I thought 'Oh my God, my God, what a bizarre name.'

"He sent me a demo, which was horrendous. *Working My Way Back To You* – awful. He then told me to watch the *Late Late Show*. It was that horrendous performance that they did and I thought 'Oh my God, what am I getting myself into?' but he just won me over somehow. He was very enthusiastic and I liked that."

Louis travelled to London with Keating and Gately to record the song. The other three band members, in what would become the normal way of doing things, didn't go to the studio.

Louis also thought Boyzone should record a version of the Monkeys *Daydream Believer*.

"Hedges' just made a magic record," says Louis. "I had the original Osmonds 45 at home and I chose *Daydream Believer* because I thought it would be a good cover and that was it."

Love Me for a Reason was released in Ireland in October 1994 and went to No. 1. Polygram in Ireland had signed the band for the world but they couldn't persuade Polydor in the UK to pick up the band and release *Love Me For A Reason* in the UK. It was extremely frustrating for the band and for Louis.

Their luck changed when Boyzone were offered a place on the *Smash Hits Roadshow* in the UK, which was a travelling showcase for new bands, along with prominent acts to pull in the crowds.

"We got on *Smash Hits Best Newcomer* and we did the seven or eight gigs around the UK and there was just a great reaction," says Louis. "They had black suits and red shirts and when they went on stage, there was just such a brilliant vibe. We had no idea what we were letting ourselves in for, in the big bad world of pop music in the UK. That was the start of it. That was the turning point."

How Boyzone ended up on the *Smash Hits* tour is unclear. Ronan Keating in his autobiography, stated that Michelle Hockley, who organised the tour, "loved" their single and called Louis. Paul Keogh says Louis met and got to know Hockley and the band somehow ended up on the tour. Mark Frith, the former editor of *Smash Hits*, says he received a plastic package with a photo of the band, a copy of the single and video and "decided that day to put them on the *Smash Hits* show".

Whatever happened, Boyzone went on tour and suddenly found themselves playing to audiences of up to 25,000 around the UK, rather than the few-dozen strong audiences they had been used to in Ireland.

Boyzone's participation in the *Smash Hits Roadshow* was a huge boost for Louis. Boyzone's inclusion on the tour silenced many of his detractors in the Irish music industry.

Shortly afterwards, the band won the *Best Newcomer* award. The winners of the *Best Newcomer* award got to appear on the *Smash Hits* Poll Winners' Party, which was televised to an audience of over 11 million on the BBC.

The Boyzone members, most likely unaware of the backroom maneouvers that Louis was engaging in to secure success, were elated. Duffy waved at the camera and said, "Everybody at home, we made it." When *Hot Press* asked why he said this, he explained: "For two reasons. One was like two fingers to all the critics and begrudgers who put us down and said we'd never do it. So, I was saying 'fuck it, we did bleedin' make it'. And I was saying to me mates and family too, 'isn't this great?'"

For Louis, it was great. There was an added bonus; the band's appearance on the show, along with the *Best Newcomer* award, drove *Love Me For A Reason* to No. 2 in the UK charts. It sold over 700,000 copies and also made the top 10 in most European countries. Boyzone was officially a success.

"I had no idea how big it was going to be. I just thought it was great. We might get a top 20 record in the UK. Fantastic. It went to No. 2. East 17 were at No. 1 with *Stay Another Day*," says Louis.

Although Mark Frith may not have been the person who engineered Boyzone's acceptance onto the *Smash Hits* Roadshow, he was the person who decided to put them on the cover of the magazine. He says he had been rooting for Louis and the band for some time, after reading about them in *Hot Press*.

"Before I met him, I kind of noticed that *Hot Press* was so pro-rock, and the cooler side of music, that they had, not an anti-Louis campaign, but they were kind of disparaging of the guy at times," says Frith.

"He got a lot of criticism because Ireland is home-grown rock music, or home-grown roots influenced music, and really this guy was seen as someone who was bringing these English or American boyband ways into the culture and had a lot of stick. I always love the under-dog, so I immediately became a fan because the poor guy was trying to do this thing in the face of adversity," adds Frith.

While Boyzone performed at the *Smash Hits* Awards, Frith and his team were putting the finishing touches to the magazine's awards issue. They had decided that Boyzone should feature on the cover, with the headline *"The Six Days That Made Them Famous!"* When the design work was completed, Frith decided to take a photocopy of the cover with him to the aftershow party.

"This was a real breakthrough for a band that had been slagged off back in Ireland," he says. "Given the incredible false start on the *Late Late Show*. I remember taking down this photocopy of the cover to show Ronan and the band, and to show Louis. They formed around me and they wanted to keep the photocopy of the cover. Louis was all bear hugs and was so, so proud that they had done it. For him, *Smash Hits* was all. *Smash Hits* meant everything. *Smash Hits* represented British music so it was a real symbol for him of having made it in Britain, and having shown people that he could do it, the fact they got on the cover of *Smash Hits*. And that was quite an amazing moment and it was great to be there at that moment."

Ensuring the band kept their feet firmly on the ground had worked. Making the front page of *Smash Hits* and winning the award reaffirmed his commitment to music. This was a different type of success to that Louis had experienced with Logan, Martin and the Eurovision. It reinforced his own belief that he was making all the right decisions and that he was right not to be swayed by criticism.

"We didn't get anything for nothing," says Keating. "We worked hard and we reaped the rewards. He always said be nice to everyone on the way up because you meet them on the way down. These were some of Louis' phrases and feelings about how Boyzone would make it. And it was down to hard work, it really was. Louis definitely pushed us and helped us to realise that."

Having his charges appear on the cover of the UK's leading pop magazine undoubtedly meant a huge amount to Louis. As a pop fanatic, he had read *Smash Hits* for years. This was the turning point in his career.

Of course, he couldn't have done it on his own. The increasing success of Boyzone entailed more administration. Louis didn't have an office filled with staff, preferring to operate on the go, with his mobile phone glued to his ear, but he did have two very able partners in Reynolds and Keogh.

Keogh explains the division of labour in the management team. "At the time, Louis had all the ideas in terms of the songs and covers and what the guys should do. But he hadn't got a clue in terms of the marketing and image and that sort of thing. So I suppose, I did all that side of it, trying to see if I could get stylists, choreographers, try to get them to look slightly different to other boybands. John Reynolds was really trying to manage the money side of it. As it grew, John took on the promoters and the merchandise, so John would always deal with the likes of Aiken or MCD, and he'd also deal with the licensees in terms of Boyzone merchandise," says Keogh.

"And Louis would then really do the links with the producers on the songs, and the publicity – well, what I would call the tabloid publicity. We would try and plan the single, launch it, promote it, get the guys to do all the personal appearances, arrange all the international travel for them, mind them, get them out of bed, get them to *Top of the Pops*."

Not only did Boyzone make the cover of *Smash Hits*, but they were also asked to go on *Top of the Pops*, the other arbiter of pop success in the UK.

"I remember arriving at *Top of the Pops* at 9 o'clock in the morning and not leaving until 12 o'clock that night. These days it's different, we turn up for two hours and we leave. But we were a bunch of kids excited about being on *Top of the Pops* and we ended up spending the day there," says Keating.

On leaving the BBC studio, a producer stopped Louis and asked if he could bring his own security the next time Boyzone came on the show. *Top of the Pops* had not expected to find swarms of screaming girls waiting out-side for a little-known boyband.

Tempting as it might have been to let their new found fame go to their heads, the members of Boyzone were never allowed to start behaving like rock stars.

As Boyzone went from strength to strength, Louis went out of his way to ensure that the impact of the fame didn't affect them for long. He had no formal training in band management or business, but he knew it was critical that Keating and his fellow band members should remain level headed.

If the band members egos ever threatened to become inflated, Louis brought them straight back down to earth.

"I remember one night we were down in the Point and we were in the dressing room. *Love Me For A Reason* had become a big hit and I think the guys actually thought they had arrived," recalls Reynolds.

"They were there and they were kind of throwing a few shapes in the dressing rooms. Suddenly Louis arrives in and says, 'John was telling me you're throwing shapes. You want to see who your fucking fans are? You want to see who's buying your fucking records?'

"He came out and he opened the boot of my car and the boot was full of CDs that we had bought. 'They're your fucking fans,' said Louis. That actually happened at the back door of the Point Depot. It is true."

Boyzone were pop stars and were advised by Louis to remain cheerful and well-behaved all the time, in public at least. "Louis set us up for these things. We were kids. We hadn't got a clue. Louis didn't have much of a clue either, but he told us what they were about and how to react and how to treat the people. It definitely helped us. There was never a bad word said about Boyzone. That was the great thing about being in the band. People always wanted us back," says Keating.

Niall Stokes of *Hot Press* believes the moulding of young band members by Louis into polite pop stars, who would always sign autographs, pose for another picture or answer another question about their favourite colour, is the "single most important thing" in his success.

"Louis had a few very good instincts," says Stokes. "Louis decided that the way to progress was to be nice to people. It was very simple and very basic but it's also very smart and very effective; in an industry that is full of people who are far too big for their own boots, and who are self-important and painful to be around. Instead of that, when Boyzone started doing their PAs, their initial radio stuff and press stuff, in the UK in particular, they were just very nice and very genuine and people thought 'We will give them a hand. We will respond positively rather than not.'

"I would say that is certainly one of the most important factors behind the success of the artists that Louis has championed. In the first instance, he made the decision with Boyzone that they would be really nice to people – and he would be too. He is a charmer and he turned it on very effectively. They weren't very good at the start and it took a lot of faith to get them to the stage where they could even hope to compete. To use a sporting metaphor, they got record company support, they got the support of *Smash Hits*, against the head. I'm not saying being nice was the only factor in securing that, but it certainly was a factor."

8

THE BOYZ NEXT DOOR

Louis envisioned Boyzone as a band in the classic boy-next-door mould, and the boy next door never forgets to say please and thank you. So Boyzone were always polite in public. Behind the scenes, however, the band found themselves under immense pressure. Some complained frequently of tiredness and fatigue.

"My abiding memory of them is that they were always tired and always overworked; no matter how many times you said to them, 'It'll all be gone in five years, guys, so you might as well work seven days a week'," says Keogh.

"Most people would give their right arm to be in that position but they generally were, I wouldn't say ungrateful, but they hadn't got the stamina."

In Keogh's opinion, Keating was the band member who took the most professional approach, even though he was the youngest.

"While the others were sometimes homesick, Ronan would have a look at something, ask if it was important to do and then get off his bum and go and do it. The others I don't think understood what was happening around them in general. They didn't understand the business, didn't understand royalties, whereas Ronan took the time to ask the questions, find out what it's all about and I suppose that's how he came to the fore. He was the youngest yet the one who looked the most clued-in."

At the time, Louis acknowledged that Boyzone believed they were working too hard. He was unsympathetic, however. He had never tasted success on this scale before, and he believed that if the band stopped working for even a short period of time, Boyzone would just collapse. He did not always practise what he preached. He was often late for appointments and had a tendency to disappear from contact for a little while.

"Louis is not very good at getting up too early," says Ray Hedges, who recalls waiting in Keogh's office on Aungier Street in Dublin with industry officials for Louis to turn up.

"On one occasion, we were sitting there, waiting for him to arrive and we just looked out the window and saw this poster. Paul Keogh had this big poster, 'Where's Louis?' hanging on Aungier St. I remember the actual moment. It was just hysterical," says Hedges. "He's not a morning person but he would always turn up just at the last second, completely dishevelled. He was always going missing."

Louis relied heavily on John Reynold's support during those years. Although he was experienced in the show business industry, he was still learning the ropes of international pop band management. The criticism directed at him by the music industry in Ireland spurred him to succeed but he was secretly still unsure of himself.

"I used to go into meetings with him and he would say, 'John, just back me on this' because he would get told off by people in record companies, saying 'I'm not sure about this and I'm not sure about that'," says Reynolds.

"For me personally, it was a massive learning experience. You were dealing with things and with people that you had never dealt with before. You were on this crest of a wave. Louis was learning. He was, at that stage, finding out how good he really was, in terms of his A&R ability. Let's be honest, we were just making it up as we went along," adds Reynolds.

To their credit, Louis and Reynolds would seek advice on the best way forward from associates they trusted.

"Jim Aiken gave me a lot of advice," says Reynolds. "We had a very good guy in charge of all the money and business affairs, an accountant called Alan McEvoy, and a lawyer, Richard Bray. I don't think anybody let egos run away with themselves, because we all realised that it was a learning expedition and we were very lucky. This was working in spite of us rather than because of us."

Louis and Paul Keogh always had a tumultuous professional relationship and both now believe the other made mistakes where Boyzone was concerned.

"Keogh made a major, major mistake," says Louis. "He wanted to control us. He wanted to be the star, whereas I wanted the five boys to be the stars. He was very good, but we were trying to control him as well. He used to have meetings in his office, where he would rant and rave about all sorts of things except making the actual pop records. He wasn't a music man. He was a marketing man. He wanted to control everybody.

"He wanted to be the boss and he didn't like me getting friendly with anybody in the office. Paul did not want that. He did not want us getting friendly with them," says Louis. "We called him 'God' on good days. We called him a lot of other things behind his back."

Boyzone's management did not only have to deal with their charges, they also had to deal with their parents, as most of the boys were so young. As the band members were receiving less than £200 each as a weekly wage, plus more for performances, their parents voiced concerns about their contracts.

"We had to deal with five sets of parents, which wasn't the easiest either," says Keogh. "Louis always ducked out of the hard decisions at the time, so we had parents thinking they were rock star managers. Louis would tell them 'They've no money because the record company won't give them any money' and they didn't understand that you don't get your royalties until you sell the damn thing. So if you're on *Top of the Pops* and you're No. 1, there's a bit of a time delay between that and the album sales and then your royalties.

"I didn't want to explain to them that it was really Louis they should be ringing. Louis would ring me and say 'Ah I had to. They were giving me a headache. I told them to ring Keogh. He has the money'."

After 1994, Keogh would rarely have to field calls from concerned parents as Boyzone became more successful than he, Reynolds, or Louis ever imagined. Boyzone earned millions in royalties and profits from concerts and merchandise. In December 1994, the band appeared twice on *Top of the Pops* and played their first sold-out concert in Dublin's Point Theatre. Louis was now one of the most respected managers in pop music.

There were times behind the scenes that he was operating on a wing and a prayer. Boyzone came under constant attack from music critics who alleged they didn't sing live. On one occasions, they were nearly caught out when their sound equipment broke in the middle of a gig.

"There was a scenario at a gig where they were playing to a backing tape. They [the fans] were screaming for an encore but the DAT machine broke, and we had to rewind the DAT machine with a pencil, because the rewind broke on it. It took the guys 15 or 20 minutes to do an encore of one song purely because we were rewinding the DAT with a fucking pencil," says Reynolds.

"If you saw it in a movie, you'd say 'that wouldn't happen in reality' but it does, and it did. I remember the time when Louis was sitting down with the pencil rewinding the fucking thing and it was surreal. I'm not trying to portray that it was amateur or anything. I'm just talking about actual situations and incidents that happened. The general public see this highly polished five-piece on stage yet behind the scenes . . . it's things like that, that kept your feet on the ground because it did create an almost surreal feel to the whole thing," says Reynolds.

"On the outside of everything, there's a very professional sheen and there's a PR machine that's behind it all. That's not real life. What you see in *OK, Hello* and *Smash Hits*, that's not real life. Real life is what really happens and I suppose it's the manager's job and the record company's job to keep that in check and play it down and portray this other image."

But success didn't just happen with Boyzone. Louis, Reynolds and Keogh worked hard. They did not expect the band to slow down once they had scored a No. 2 single in the UK. Louis also maintained the pace he had set for himself.

"Louis built up his own contacts through hard work," says Keogh. "Louis was out every night of the week, hanging around *Smash Hits* parties, [and] got to know everybody very quickly, which is what a manager should do." Not everyone would regard hanging around at parties as hard work, but it is one of a pop band manager's many responsibilities.

Boyzone went from strength to strength. In April 1995, *Key To My Life*, written by Graham, Keating, and Gately with help from Ray Hedges, reached No. 3 in the UK, as did their next single *So Good*, released in July. Boyzone then had to hit the road to promote their forthcoming album.

Louis decided that Boyzone should complete a gruelling tour of Ireland, where they played 36 concerts in 30 days. They then toured the UK, winding up with a concert in London's Royal Albert Hall in October 1995. By the end, they were exhausted but Louis was right – the hard work paid off.

When the album *Said and Done* was released in the UK, it went to No. 1 and eventually sold over 1.5 million copies around the world. The band's fourth UK single was Keating's old favourite, *Father and Son*. Released in November 1995, it reached No. 2 in the charts. With four top 5 hits in a year, Boyzone had become a household name in the UK.

But they still had not reached No. 1, however, and they didn't get one with their next single either. *Coming Home Now*, released in March 1996, reached No. 1. *Coming Home Now* was notable for a different reason. It was released at the same time as Take That's last single *How Deep Is Your Love*. Take That had been the premier boyband in the UK for some years but now that they had split, their place in teenage hearts was there for the taking.

Boyzone's management reacted quickly and the group's second album, *A Different Beat*, was released in October 1996. It went straight in at No. 1. The first single from the album, a cover of the Bee Gees song *Words*, which Louis had suggested Boyzone should cover, also reached No. 1, selling over 400,000 copies. Boyzone were the new kings of pop.

A Different Beat was a more slickly produced affair than the group's first album. Hedges took care of most of the production and brought in several other top name producers: Rick Wake, who had worked with Celine Dion, and would later produce hits for Jennifer Lopez.; Jeremy Wheatley, who had produced for Tom Jones and the Spice Girls, and would later work with S Club 7; Phil Harding, who had been a producer on albums by the Pet Shop Boys and Erasure; and, the Irish songwriter, Phil Coulter.

The album generated three more hit singles, *A Different Beat* (No. 1), *Isn't It A Wonder* (No. 1), and *Picture Of You* (No. 2), which was included on the second release of the album, and on their subsequent album, after Ronan Keating won an Ivor Novello award for penning the song.

As Louis finalised preparations to release *A Different Beat*, Boyzone embarked on yet more hectic touring. One incident led Paul Keogh to believe disaster had struck.

In the spring of 1996, Boyzone were touring the Far East. By the time, they reached Japan, tour fatigue had set in. A huge row erupted between the band members and they announced to their entourage that they were going to split up.

"Louis never travelled with them," says Keogh. "They [Boyzone] had a row, and someone who worked for Polygram in Ireland at the time rang me and said:

'The band is about to break up.' So I had to get on a flight and go to Japan. Of course, they heard I was on the way. Louis rang them saying, 'God', as they called me, 'God is on the way' so of course by the time I get to Tokyo, the row is over, and I said to them, 'Bloody eejits, 24-hour trip to Tokyo'."

Asked about it, Ronan Keating sounds indignant. "I've never seen Paul Keogh in Tokyo in my life. That's waffle."

One thing is true. Keogh was called 'God' by Louis and the band, presumably because he was the disciplinarian in the Boyzone set-up.

"Louis was too soft on them," he says. "They had Louis wrapped around their fingers. They didn't show up for TV appearances, and I was the one then that would have to read the Riot Act." Keogh says he also found it particularly irritating that the band members did not appear to appreciate their luck in seeing the world.

"They never seemed to appreciate the travel element. They always thought it was a chore. For some kids, it would have been brilliant to go to Australia, travelling business class, going into lounges, drinking most of the trolley, going on the flight, getting off it, getting into limos. They even had armed guards in Singapore from the steps of the plane right into their hotel. They all thought it was a chore. The real chore was for people like me that travelled with them," he says.

While the band may have seemed ungrateful for the opportunities they received, it is not difficult to understand their weary complaints. Having completed their tour of the Far East, they set off on another tour of the UK in the summer of 1996, playing four sold-out gigs in Wembley Stadium.

Once the album was released, they had to engage in constant promotional work to boost sales. There was scarcely a gap in their schedules. Louis remained convinced, and rightly so, that the key to Boyzone's success was hard work.

Boyzone became a worldwide phenomenon. The band had risen to prominence under Louis' direction. Keating and Boyzone followed Louis' instructions precisely and respected his advice. "He was," said Keating, "the sixth member of the band."

There are band managers who try to be too authoritative, issuing unreasonable demands and ultimatums that cause their act to fight back and rebel. Louis didn't make this mistake. He made Boyzone believe he was one of them. And that they were fighting against the record company.

In early 1997, Boyzone headed off on tour to South East Asia, the Middle East and India, all areas where they had built up a huge following. The tour of South East Asia caused the group unexpected consternation. When the details of the tour were released, it was noticed that Boyzone intended to perform in Indonesia. The group was promptly embroiled in political controversy. At the time, Indonesia was conducting genocide in East Timor.

Large numbers of Irish people protested, encouraged by the East Timor Solidarity Campaign, and demanded that Boyzone withdraw from the planned concerts in Indonesia. As the contracts had been signed, the concerts went ahead as scheduled but both Boyzone and Louis were heavily criticised for the decision. It was not one of Louis' finer moments.

The tour was also notable as the band experienced extreme fan mania for the first time. Thousands of fans thronged the airports of places like Manila in the

Philippines and Surabaya in Indonesia. The band were mobbed wherever they went, and frequently had to stop concerts briefly as fans at the front were crushed.

Meanwhile in Ireland, Louis and Paul Keogh parted ways. After Boyzone's second No. 1 album, and another spate of hit singles, Polydor in the UK had begun to show a deep interest in Boyzone. Louis and Keogh had always had a tempestuous working relationship.

"Louis and I were still barking at each other," recalls Keogh. Louis also knew Polydor in the UK had more influential connections than Polygram. This fact was also at the back of his mind.

"The way I looked at it was, I'd done it now for three years at this stage, and I thought: 'Well, we have them signed, so why not get Polydor UK to do all the work, and I'll still get the royalties'," says Keogh.

"I was sick of travelling at that stage and to be honest with you, we at the Irish office would have had little or no dealings with them, but would still take money. So, it was a very profitable signing in the end for Polygram Ireland.

"It was one of the few acts that the actual record company royalties came into Ireland. U2's artist royalties obviously come into Principle Management [owned by Paul McGuinness] but the record royalties would have gone to Island Records, nowhere near Ireland. So, we were the first record company to make a couple of million at least [out of Boyzone], so it was a very profitable time."

While Keogh is critical of Boyzone in certain ways, he remembers his time working with the band with great fondness. He liked Boyzone, Reynolds and Louis.

"Every time somebody says 'Boyzone' to me I do actually laugh. That's my first reaction because they were very funny. The one thing you couldn't take away from them, that English acts hadn't got, was that they had a great sense of humour and they had a great sense of devilment.

"They'd be tired and the next thing somebody would crack a joke and they'd be off again, and they'd wake up and they'd be gone messing. But they were, as somebody once said, 'never dull, never boring, but never content' and I thought that summed them up."

Louis always believed Keogh had worked against him, and not with him but says Boyzone wouldn't have happened without Keogh's involvement.

"I was always into making the music and getting the acts, and if he had stuck to the marketing and stopped trying to control people, I think he would be in the music business now. He could have been very big in the music business but he did it his way," says Louis.

Keogh, however, is unabashed about his handling of Boyzone and Louis.

"There was nobody in the world wanted a boyband from Ireland. We would never have got off the ground if we had rules and didn't do all the things we did do."

The head of A&R in Polydor in the UK, Colin Barlow, took Keogh's place. Louis had previously attempted to involve Polydor in Boyzone through Lucian Grainge, the head of Universal Music in the UK. Grainge is reputed to be the most powerful man in the UK music industry but Louis' first attempt to bring him on board failed.

"Someone in our promotion department said Boyzone, this Irish group, were coming over and they were doing the *Smash Hits* tour," recalls Grainge.

"I rang him up and said 'there's a very good reaction and some of my people are going down to see you on the *Smash Hits* tour. I think we had another group on there at the time. He said, 'No, we don't want to sign to Polygram. We want to be on London.'

"So I said, 'Well, you can't be on London because we're going to release you. You're signed to Polygram in Ireland. So he said, 'No, no, no, you don't get it. We're going to sign to London' and I said, 'Well, no, you're not'. So I hated him."

Barlow, like Grainge, was a heavyweight in the industry, one of only two British A&R people in the global A&R top 20. He said Louis made the first approach. "Louis came to me when the second album was finished," recalls Barlow.

"I started to get involved, and then kind of got slowly but surely moved into being the A&R person totally for Boyzone and made the third album. I put that whole thing together with Louis, and that was when I got heavily involved in Boyzone."

Although Louis and Boyzone had already experienced pop success on a grand scale, Barlow believed he could take them further. "I think the key was what Boyzone hadn't done on the first two albums was sell records outside the UK and my role really was to take it up a gear. Luckily, it did."

Barlow went about "taking it up a gear" by bringing in high profile songwriters and producers to work on Boyzone's third album, *Where We Belong*.

He sought the services of Mark Hudson and Mike Mancini, who worked with Bon Jovi and Hanson; Steve Lipson, who produced songs for Annie Lennox and Whitney Houston, and Denniz Pop and Per Magnusson of the Swedish song factory Cheiron. He also hired Diana Warren, who had written songs for Celine Dion.

Barlow's instincts were correct. *Where We Belong* went straight into the UK charts at No. 1 when it was released in August 1998. Two singles from the album also made No. 1 (*All That I Need* and *No Matter What*), and two others made it to No. 1 (*Baby Can I Hold You* and *I Love The Way You Love Me*). *No Matter What*, from the musical *Whistle Down The Wind*, was also the first Boyzone single to sell over a million copies, and it was voted the best single of 1998 in a national phone poll in the UK.

The move to Polydor in the UK also signalled renewed efforts to break Boyzone in the US. Louis remained firm in the belief that US success was no longer an ambition. He believed it could be achieved. Polydor's management was of the same opinion.

Before simply releasing their songs in America, Polydor approached Jim Steinman, the producer who co-wrote *No Matter What*. Steinman undertook the US distribution of a reworked version of *Where We Belong* on his new label Ravenous (owned by Mercury). But the record never made an impact for no clear reasons. It was well received by the critics, incredibly well received in some cases. A review in the prestigious *Rolling Stone* magazine stated: "More adventurous and genuine than 'N Sync, less contrived and pompous than the Backstreet Boys. Boyzone are bringing their choreography and Celtic charms to the last great frontier. *Where We Belong*, released in Europe nearly six months ago, exhibits Boyzone's penchant for unabashed radio candy — sticky sweet and addictive — as well as authentic musicianship and instrumentation." It continued: "Nearly all fourteen tracks — from the impeccably produced *One Kiss at a*

Time to the sincere ballad *All the Time in the World* — dare critics to do more than glance at the album cover and toss it in the trash. Boyzone are grassroots guys – they write and produce nearly all of their songs, a rare and respectable practice in the boy band industry."

Boyzone's "authentic musicianship" went unnoticed by the general public in the US.

Keogh blames Polydor for this failure. "It was the record company's fault that they never broke America," he says. "Nobody in the record company was prepared to put the money into it, because it would have taken about three to four million dollars just to take the single off the ground in America."

This unwillingness to invest in Boyzone provided the first clue that the band was on a downward slope, believes Keogh. Louis partly agrees.

"Looking back now," he says, "I don't think the band was good enough to make it in America. They didn't have enough. The vocals weren't good enough."

9

WESTSIDE STORY

Louis' accomplishments with Boyzone convincingly proved that Ireland could produce pop bands. The envious local rock fraternity in Ireland were less than effusive about his achievements. Louis was openly criticised, castigated and attacked; many of his detractors would have been happy to see his career collapse. The more he was criticised, the more he was determined to show that he could enjoy longevity as a pop manager. Partly so he would continue to succeed at his chosen profession, and partly to make sure his critics wouldn't have the last laugh, Louis maintained an almost religious devotion to finding and cultivating new talent from 1996.

He didn't need a clairvoyant to tell him that Boyzone would inevitably break up and he made plans for that eventuality. Although he was managing one of the world's biggest pop bands, which had made him a millionaire several times over, his future was not secure while Boyzone were his only act. For the time being, he had power and influence, but a rapid fall from grace would be inevitable once Boyzone broke up, unless he had more acts to unveil.

While managing Boyzone, he continued to manage small bands playing in provincial towns and around Dublin city. He constantly searched for fresh talent. He was not a man who could leave things to chance in the hope that a potential pop star would come knocking on his door. He actively kept watch for bands, singers and musicians and signed a number of acts, hoping that one could be the next international smash hit. It may seem odd that he afforded other acts his time and energy given the success of Boyzone, but he did and used the connections he made bringing Boyzone success to promote his other charges.

As early as 1994, he began recruiting new talent when he signed Who's Eddie, a pop band comprised of three sisters and a brother – Orla, Dara, Jacqui and Keith Molloy.

"We came in on the back of Boyzone," says Jacqui Molloy. "He had heard of us and there was a message to contact him, so I rang the office. I knew he'd been an agent or something, so I thought 'What the hell. I'll give him a ring. Maybe he wants girls now, if he has had boys'. He was interested, came to see the band, loved the whole vibe, was very into it."

Louis signed Who's Eddie weeks later. Under his stewardship, the band achieved a degree of success, producing three hit singles that made the top ten in the Irish charts. Another record from the band reached the top five in the British dance charts. Louis used the same management techniques with Who's Eddie that had worked so well for Boyzone. The band was signed by Polygram, Boyzone's record label. He hired reputable producers, convinced the Molloys would take off. Unfortunately, international stardom didn't happen for Who's Eddie.

"It was easy to market a boyband or a girlband. I think we were just something a little bit different, so you couldn't put us into a box, so that created all sorts of problems, even for Louis," says Molloy.

"He did what he could, but he hadn't the power that he does now. As time went on, every time you saw him, he had met somebody else, or he had got further in the music industry or met a bigger producer. He was mixing in different circles."

The band eventually decided to leave Louis' management in 1998 and turned to Carol Hanna to book their gigs.

"It wasn't so much that we decided that Carol would do the booking. It was just that he was never in the country, and he couldn't do the dates. It just sort of happened. He was so busy with everything else and he was never in the country."

The relationship ended amicably though; there were no arguments, no bitter recriminations and no harsh words exchanged.

"I think I met them too late in their career for international success," says Louis. "I couldn't get them a record deal in the UK because people would say they were too long in the tooth. Talented, but too long in the tooth. I mean, we had meetings with Warner Brothers in the UK and lots of other people, and at least Keith got a publishing deal out of it.

"I think he'll get a hit record with somebody in the UK. We haven't heard the end of him. They always had great potential but they just never got the break. They've worked very hard for everything they've got. You have to admire people like that."

With both Boyzone and Who's Eddie under his management in the mid 1990s, Louis was still eager to find more new acts. He would constantly ask his friends to watch out for talent that he could groom into the next pop sensation.

Linda Martin, with whom Louis always maintained a personal friendship, unexpectedly discovered a new act for Louis in the summer of 1996. Martin and a friend were partying in the POD, the nightclub owned by John Reynolds, when she saw twin brothers singing one of Johnny Logan's songs. She was impressed. The brothers were Tony and Steven Carter. Martin called Louis at once with news of the discovery.

"She said, 'You have to see these guys. They're great'," recalls Louis. The twin's telephone numbers were passed to Louis who arranged to meet the brothers and watch them perform. Louis agreed with Martin's analysis and decided to manage the twins, who at the time called themselves Brother 2 Brother. Louis immediately changed the pair's name to the Carter Twins and began touting them as "a young Righteous Brothers". He also decided to bring the 19-year-old Keating on board as co-manager.

"I thought they had great potential for middle of the road pop," says Louis of the Carter Twins.

Louis had always held out great hopes for Keating. He looked upon the young singer as his prodigy. Keating was the first person in Boyzone to start making plans for his future career. He had shown an interest in manage-ment, with a particular emphasis on learning to select and write songs. It was clear there was something else behind Keating's apparently innocent foray into music management. Keating was preparing for a solo career but if anyone noticed, they didn't say anything.

As Boyzone were already internationally successful, Louis had little difficulty in persuading A&R rep-resentatives in the UK to take a look at his latest pop offering. The Carter Twins were promptly signed to

RCA in London, and given a support slot touring with Boyzone.

Louis also succeeded in getting the brothers onto the 1996 *Smash Hits* Roadshow. The twins later won the *Best Newcomer* award, just as Boyzone had two years previously. Unfortunately global stardom never came their way.

The single was a cover of the old classic, *Twelfth of Never*. The single failed to achieve any notable success, peaking at a distinctly unimpressive No. 61 in the UK charts, although it did make the top 10 in Ireland.

RCA decided to be patient. Louis explored every possible avenue to success. In an effort to boost the Twins profile, RCA paid £20,000 for a support role on Peter André's UK tour, but it didn't pay off. The Carters next single failed to chart.

Louis and RCA were nonplussed by this lack of success and persisted in pushing the Carters. The twins toured Ireland in the summer of 1997 with the 2FM Beat on the Street. They were back on the *Smash Hits* Roadshow in the autumn of 1997, and they continued to support Boyzone whenever possible. All these performances failed to boost the Carter Twins public profile in any significant way.

RCA persevered and released a Carter Twins album called *Number One*, possibly one of the most unfortunately titled records of all time. It didn't perform well and failed to achieve sales forecasts.

Louis nor RCA could understand what happened. The Carters were well received whenever they toured. They were also good performers. Furthermore, their album had been produced by the respected pair of Phil Harding and Ian Curnow. Harding had produced hits for Kylie Minogue and the Pet Shop Boys among others and, along with Curnow, had written memorable pop singles such as East 17's *Stay Another Day*.

It was during this time that Louis persuaded the Carters to enter the Irish National Song Contest, the qualifying competition for the Eurovision. Louis was enthusiastic about their prospects right up until the Contest.

Paul Harrington, who played guitar with the Carters that night, remembers Louis watching over the brothers protectively. "When we were rehearsing," says Harrington, "Louis would always be there. He would always call in, even though it was at the height of Boyzone. He's always professional."

Although he maintained vociferously he "didn't care" who won, he cared enough to ensure that Keating hosted the competition, and that Boyzone performed in the interval. Keating also wrote *Make The Change* for the Carters to perform. Louis was confident that the Carter Twins would win but they didn't. They came fourth. Louis took it as a personal insult. He couldn't hide his emotions and exploded. The rock journalist George Byrne distinctly remembers hearing a lot about the injustice of it all. "He went nuts! That was the only time I've ever really seen him go baloobas," Byrne smiles. "The Eurovision kind of meant something to him. He absolutely lost the rag as a result of that. He really went mad."

Louis was particularly disgusted because the winning song didn't become an international hit, something one of his acts would probably have managed. He blamed RTE, saying that it had a great chance to create a hit record but had blown it. He offered to revamp the National Song Contest for RTE the next year, and promised that if the broadcaster went about selecting a Eurovision entrant his way, it would have a hit single on their hands in 1999. RTE chose not to rise to the challenge.

"I didn't lose my temper. If they had sent them [the Carters], they would have had a big hit record in the UK. It was always a great platform every year for somebody to get a hit record. It's all about getting somebody with star quality, a great songwriter, a big record company behind them and a manager that was prepared to work at it. I was annoyed because I thought they should have won it," he says.

RTE may be culpable in terms of failing to make Eurovision hits, but Louis made some mistakes himself where the Carter Twins were concerned. He put them into two successive pantomimes in Dublin's Gaiety Theatre. Observers say he failed to realise that when audiences see pop stars in a pantomime, they automatically think of failed pop stars. Audiences know that pantomimes are the retirement homes of showbusiness. Louis says he had no other choice and wanted the Carters to earn money.

"I was prepared to keep them going," he says. "The odd thing about me and the Carter Twins was I never put them under contract, and the oddest thing of all, is that they left me! That's the real story that nobody knows. That's exactly what happened.

"They were really nice guys, Steve and Tony, and I could have got them another record contract. I wanted to make them into another Robson and Jerome. They were great kids and they were really nice. They had great voices. A lot of people didn't like them, but I don't listen to that. I was going to keep at it with them. I was going to get them another record deal.

"Virgin were interested in them at that stage. There was a market for middle of the road. Tom Jones, Cliff

Richard, Julio Iglesias," says Louis. "Iglesias sells millions of records worldwide. Middle of the road is great. It's hard to market sometimes and it's hard to get radio. But it's a huge market." RCA dropped the brothers in September 1998.

Months before Steve and Tony Carter left Louis' management company, he received a telephone call from Mae Filan. The woman wanted to talk about her son Shane and a boyband he'd put together called IOYou. Mrs. Filan came from Kiltimagh and had already called Louis' brother about her son. She wanted a favour.

"I thought 'here we go' because I get calls like this every single day," says Louis. "I distinctly remember her telling me he was like Michael Jackson, he was great and all the rest. So I said, 'Listen, I'll meet them' so I met Shane, Kian and, I think one of the other guys from IOYou, in Dublin."

Shane Filan says now that IOYou could scarcely believe their luck. "I didn't actually believe that she had got through to him. I wouldn't believe her. She had to ring me back three times, honestly, before I would actually believe her. When I found out we were meeting him, I thought 'Oh my God, imagine if this guy actually managed us or if he got one of his assistants to manage us.' That's how much we felt about him."

While the young band members were starstruck at the prospect of meeting Louis, he was impressed by their vocal ability.

"They came to Ronan's 21st birthday party in the Red Box and the thing I liked about them was their personalities. They were really nice country guys. I mean, they looked like culchies, but when they sang, my God, it was just amazing. You just can't get voices like that anywhere. It was the voices and the attitude. They were so hungry for any kind of fame and that was the best thing about them." Louis felt sure the band had potential.

IOYou was made up of six boys who had all attended Summerhill College in Sligo: Kian Egan, Mark Feehily, Shane Filan, Micheal Garrett, Derek Lacey and Graham Keighron. They came together after performing in a school production of *Grease* and called themselves Six as One, but changed the name to IOYou. They achieved some success in Co. Sligo and performed a couple of gigs locally. Their determination and ambition was evident from the beginning. They decided to release a single, *Together Girl Forever,* on an indie label in their hometown. The cover of the single featured the six band members staring sulkily into the camera and sporting bad haircuts and ill-fitting black suits. The single was relatively successful, however, and drew some media attention, including an invitation to appear on RTE's Nationwide programme.

This moderate acclaim was thrilling for IOYou but they were aware that further success was likely to evade them without the backing of a manager who knew the business.

When Louis got involved in the project, things immediately took a turn for the better. Before he became the group's manager, he secured them a slot supporting the Backstreet Boys at a concert in Dublin on St. Patrick's Day.

"It was like a dream come true," Kian Egan told *Hot Press* three months later. "One minute we're all sitting in a room in Sligo, and the next night we're performing to over 9,000 people. We're really just five culchies coming into a pop scene in Dublin."

Louis knew IOYou contained some good singers but the Backstreet Boys gig convinced him they could also rise to the challenge of performing to big crowds. He immediately decided to manage the band.

By this time, Louis had built up an impressive network of contacts in the UK music business. He sent a message to Simon Cowell, one of Britain's most respected A&R figures. Cowell wanted to know more and Louis convinced him that IOYou was not an opportunity to be missed.

"He called me very excitedly to say he had a band, a six-piece boyband called IOYou," recalls Cowell. "I subsequently went to Ireland to meet the boys and told him to forget it. I told him in no uncertain terms that he had to lose some of the members and get in new people. He told me to forget it and he said he'd get a deal for the boys."

Louis stood his ground much to the relief of the band's members.

"He told me to change three of them and one of the people he told me to change was Shane," he says. Louis believed that Shane had all the necessary qualities to be in a boyband but was irate at what he perceived as a lack of professionalism on the young singer's part.

"The first time we auditioned for Simon Cowell, I looked just like I didn't care. I wasn't dressed well. I didn't sing well. I was very nervous and I just didn't fit the bill in Simon Cowell's eyes. Louis couldn't believe it. He was really disgusted with me that day and it was the first fight I had with Louis. He really gave out to me. He took me to one side and said, 'Listen, you've got to cop on. Don't ever do that again. Have some respect.' I just thought everything, all my dreams were over, that he was going to say good luck to me," remembers Filan.

Despite his anger, Louis decided to keep Filan in the group. He knew, however, that he would have to heed Cowell's advice to some extent if IOYou were ever to get a record deal. He asked Derek Lacey to leave the band because he didn't fit in.

In reality, the move was part of a well thought out plan to turn IOYou into a financially viable product. Louis always had a formula for the ideal boyband.

The package worked best if teenage girls, the core of any boyband's fanbase, regarded the band's members as boy-next-door types. "The girls must believe in the backs of their minds that one day they'll go out with him," he says.

Louis next changed the band's name to Westside. Through his contacts, he arranged for Westside to appear on the *Beat on the Street*, the Irish version of the *Smash Hits* Roadshow, that July. The band were next dispatched to London to record two tracks with well-known pop producer, Steve Mac, who had worked with Boyzone.

Westside were never going to perform in pubs and parish halls. Louis was now respected and humoured rather than tolerated or ignored. After the recording session, Louis concluded that Graham Keighron did not fit in and asked him to leave the band. Keighron accepted Louis' judgment but he remained friends with the band, particularly with Kian, and later accompanied the band on tour.

A boyband with four members didn't fit Louis' notion of a perfect formula. Coincidentally, just as Louis needed another member for the band, he was made aware of auditions being held by another manager called Noel Carty. He was putting together a traditional music boyband that would eventually become Reel.

Louis found two singers at these auditions – Nicky Byrne and Bryan McFadden. Byrne performed regularly with his father Nicholas, who had a band called Nikki and Studz. McFadden had attended the Billie Barry stage school and been in another pop band called Cartel, so both possessed stage experience. From Louis' pers-pective, both had a look he was after.

Westside had gone from having six members to five to four, and now it had six again. Louis was still unhappy. He only wanted five. Michael Garrett was promptly dropped from the line up. Unlike Keighron, he took the rejection badly and returned home to Sligo dispirited. His shattered dream didn't weigh on Louis' mind. He had succeeded in shaping the band to fit his formula and now he had work to do.

Louis' ruthless shaping of the band was hard to cope with for the three remaining original members.

"It was very difficult because they were like our three best friends in the band," recalls Filan. "The six of us were very close at the time. He didn't feel that three of them fitted the band or weren't right for him in his eyes. It was very hard but we had the decision to go with the most talked about manager in Ireland to make our dreams come true. We knew straight away any one of us, no matter who it was, would have gone for it. I don't think any of the lads in Sligo now could say they wouldn't have gone for it if it was their choice. Because it was the chance of a lifetime."

In the five years after Louis had touted photos of Boyzone to anyone and everyone he could think of, his circumstances had changed. Louis had proved he could cut it as a band manager and this time around, the record companies were falling over themselves to sign his latest ensemble. A&R representatives from BMG, Polydor, Parlophone, Virgin and MCA all met with Louis and the band. Three offered Westside a contract. In the end, Simon Cowell of RCA, owned by BMG, succeeded in signing the band in October 1998. The contract was for £4 million.

Although Cowell didn't realise it at the time, Louis had played a trick on him. He was anxious to keep Filan in the group but wanted Cowell to believe he had done as instructed and asked Filan to leave. Louis' solution was typical of his ingenuity and nerve. He told Filan to grow his hair long and dye it blond, so Cowell would not recognise him when he came back to Dublin to see the group at a showcase in the Red Box.

"I said 'Oh God, this is never going to work.' When Simon came back, I had long blond hair. I got up and sang and Simon Cowell was like 'Who's the new guy? He's great!' and Louis said 'That's the guy I got for you. That's the new guy!' We got a record deal then. Simon laughs about it now," says Filan.

Cowell acknowledges that the stunt was funny but is unapologetic about his initial views about Filan's involvement in the band. His strategy at the time was to exert pressure on Louis to make the band leaner and more likely to succeed.

"In the end, we both kind of got our own way, because he got Shane to dye his hair blond and snuck him in! But when I saw the band it only took me thirty seconds to turn around to him and say, 'We have a deal'," says Cowell.

"They looked better. They were very tight. They weren't so nervous and it was just one of those great showcases you go to once every 10 years and everything about this band told me they were going to be successful."

Boyzone's creative director and friend of Louis', Colin Barlow of Polydor, had wanted to sign Westlife but was stopped by Lucian Grainge. He had grave reservations about Louis' plans. "That is true and if I had my time over again I wouldn't have done that," says Grainge. "I had three things on my mind at the time. One was making sure that the next Boyzone album got the best possible shot, and then I believed that out of Boyzone, we would launch Ronan as a solo artist and also Stephen Gately, and that at some point we would have a Greatest Hits. So I took the view that there were four prospects there that I needed to protect in the long term. Certainly over the forthcoming two or three years: Ronan, Stephen, the Boyzone album and all the touring and all the international work and so forth as well as obviously the Greatest Hits.

"Colin was desperate to sign Westlife. I kept saying to him, 'It is a junior version of Boyzone. You're going to kill Boyzone internally overnight' and it was not in anyone's interest to extinguish Boyzone prematurely. I also felt that the only way in which you could break Westlife, was that if you attacked Boyzone, if you completely went for their audience, their market, their techniques, everything and I wasn't prepared to do that," says Grainge.

"And in reality, that's exactly unfortunately what happened. When they signed to BMG, it was a complete carbon copy. And I also think that at the time Ronan co-managed them. Louis gave Ronan a piece of the management, I think I probably look back on it and think there may have been something, either conscious or sub-conscious, that maybe Ronan actually wanted to break from Boyzone, so he could get on with his own career," adds Grainge.

Even before the contract with Cowell was signed, Westside had supported Boyzone on their European tour in September and October. Parachuting the new act in as support to his established band was the cheapest and most effective way to reach thousands of potential fans quickly. With the contract signed, Westside were then sent off on the *Smash Hits* Roadshow, and they duly won the *Best Newcomer* award, like Boyzone had four years earlier. Despite having performed in public on a number of occasions, the band had still not been officially launched. The band spent the next few months with a singing coach, a dietician, and stylists before they were ready to be presented to the press. A showcase gig was organised for the band in the Café de Paris in London. In less than a year, Westside had been transformed into a slick pop band.

There was one problem. It was brought to the attention of RCA that there were eight other groups on the National Band Register with Westside in their names. The legal advice RCA obtained led to the band being re-named Westlife – their fourth and final name.

From this point onwards, it was pretty much a given that Westlife would be a success, but nothing was left to chance. They were coached in every aspect of the pop star life. They had the backing of a major UK label, and the experience of Louis to guide them forward. They also had Ronan Keating, who had been co-opted as Westlife's "co-manager". A company called Rolo Management was formed to oversee the business. Keating continued as their co-manager for about a year.

The main reason for having Keating as co-manager, given that Louis was not a household name at this time, seems to have been to provide added publicity for the launch of the new band. It was also clearly intended to boost Keating's credibility. Since then, many have doubted if Ronan had anything to do with the running of Westlife at all, but Louis maintains that he did. Asked if Keating really co-managed the band, Louis replies: "He was a mentor. He was good to give them advice. He was like a sixth member of the band for a while and he was very honest with them about different things and they looked up to him."

Louis and Keating weren't the only people involved with the group. To ensure that Westlife were given the best possible chance of conquering the charts, the heavy-weights of pop production and songwriting were brought on board.

On their eponymously titled first album, released in November 1999, the band continued to work with Steve Mac and his songwriting partner, Wayne Hector at Steve Mac's Rokstone Studios. Jôrgen Elofsson, David Kreuger, Per Magnusson, Max Martin and Rami of the Swedish studio Cheiron also weighed in with their contribution, while Pete Waterman produced the album, which eventually reached No. 2 in the albums chart.

Westlife's first single, *Swear It Again,* was released in March 1999 and went straight to No. 1 in the UK, staying there for two weeks, beating both Fatboy Slim and The Offspring to the top spot. It was to be the first of four No. 1 singles for the band that year, with *If I Let You Go* in at the top in August, followed by *Flying Without Wings* in October and the double A-side of cover versions, *I Have A Dream/Seasons In The Sun,* in December. This last number one sold 213,000 copies and deprived Sir Cliff Richard of his customary Christmas No. 1.

Westlife were only the second act ever to have their first four singles reach the top of the charts. B*Witched had managed the same feat in the previous year. They were also Irish, counting two of Shane Lynch's sisters among their number, but they were not managed by Louis Walsh, who had passed the band to Ray Hedges. When Westlife's fifth single, and the last to be released from their first album *Fool Again*, went to No. 1 in April 2000, they became the first band ever to have their first five singles go straight in at the top. In the first year of record sales, Westlife had already outperformed Boyzone, who only got to No. 1 with their sixth single.

It had proven to be an astonishingly successful year. Apart from all the No. 1s, Westlife also won the Best UK & Ireland Act from MTV in November and ITV's Record Of The Year for *Flying Without Wings*. The band, and its management, had scarcely put a foot wrong. They did attract a little controversy in November 1999 when they agreed to launch the annual British Legion Poppy Appeal. Sinn Féin protested vigorously, saying it was "insensitive in the extreme" and that Westlife should not support a "British military charity". The Ulster Unionists countered, defending the boyband's actions and accusing Sinn Féin of mounting "a silly outdated" protest.

RCA moved quickly to quash the controversy, saying the Poppy Appeal decision had been theirs and it would stand. Westlife went ahead and launched the appeal.

10

SEPARATE LIVES

L ouis had announced on more than one occasion that Boyzone were on the verge of splitting, but it had never been more than a publicity ruse. As Lynch told the tabloids: "We're sick and tired of reading that we're going to split up, and the fact that it's our manager who keeps putting out the stories really winds us up. He's a complete berk, and only does it when he thinks we need help shifting concert tickets. I don't think we've done a concert for the past five years that hasn't sold out."

In March 1999, Boyzone secured another No. 1 in the UK with a cover of the Billy Ocean song *When The Going Gets Tough*, which they recorded for Comic Relief. Westlife simultaneously entered the charts and got their first UK No. 1. Boyzone realised Louis' full attention was no longer focused on them. The band had two further hits in 1999, *You Needed Me* (No. 1) and *Every Day I Love You* (No. 3). These were both taken from the group's fourth album *By Request*, a greatest hits compilation released at the end of May. The greatest hits album was destined to be Boyzone's last but the band members could be excused for not realising this; the album outsold every other record released in the UK that year.

In spite of the limited musical capability of some members of the group, Paul Keogh believes Boyzone came to believe they should have more influence over the direction of the group.

"As they got more powerful, they started to push their own views and they made a lot of mistakes because they forgot who their audience was," says Keogh.

"It's hard for boybands to realise that the vast majority of their audience are probably seven and eight years of age. So trying to look sexy and all that just goes straight over these kid's heads. They just want to sing along to *Father and Son* and they want to see Ronan scream and smile. It's all pantomime, more than music business."

The biggest indicator that Boyzone was about to collapse came in July of the same year when Keating released his first solo record, a cover of the Keith Whitley song *When You Say Nothing At All*. The song was recorded for inclusion on the soundtrack of the film *Notting Hill*. It reached No. 1 and Keating distinctly enjoyed the rush of being a solo performer.

The single's success and the way Keating relished his achievement should have sounded alarm bells for the rest of the group, but it didn't. They were otherwise preoccupied in the summer of 1999.

Despite Louis' instructions that girlfriends be kept out of sight, both Duffy and Graham fathered children with their long-term girlfriends, while Keating and Lynch married theirs. With four of the band publicly "taken", only one was left to fend off questions about his personal life.

Gately was homosexual and in a relationship with Eloy de Jong, a member of Dutch boyband Caught In

The Act, but this relationship had been kept from the media. Louis himself believed Gately was entitled to his private life. An unexpected problem, however, presented itself that summer when a former security guard attempted to sell Gately's story to the English tabloids. Louis was deeply worried for Gately's sake. Although there had been plenty of gay boyband members in the past, none of them had ever been openly gay.

"I didn't know when he joined the band that he was gay," says Louis. "I had no idea at all. It would have been a big thing to me at the time, because I thought it would have been very damaging. But it wasn't. Everybody in the media knew he was gay and nobody cared.

"I think it was best for him to get it out of himself because he was the one with the problem. Nobody else had the problem except Stephen. When he came out in *The Sun*, we didn't get one bad letter. He didn't lose any fans as a result. I think he was a better person. He was a happier person."

Gately officially became gay on 16 June that year when *The Sun* published "Boyzone Stephen: I'm Gay And I'm In Love" on page one. Gately received thousands of supportive emails and letters from fans, along with a letter from Graham Norton, flowers from Elton John, and a phone call from George Michael. The readers of *Smash Hits* voted him "Hero of the Year".

Having seen out the storm, Louis and the rest of the band were soon to experience more upheaval. By December 1999, the tabloids and celebrity gossip magazines had more fodder for their pages. Buoyed by the success of *When You Say Nothing At All*, Keating announced that he wanted to take a break and work on an album of his own.

Duffy and Lynch, in particular, were unhappy to go along with this plan, but without their lead singer, the group could scarcely continue. Boyzone formally announced they were taking a break for a year. Everyone in the band, including Keating, appears to have believed the band was on sabbatical. The music industry, the media and the fans accepted that Boyzone was finished.

Under Louis' stewardship, Boyzone was one of the most successful boybands ever. They had 16 top three singles, six of which were No. 1s. They had four No. 1 albums, selling over 12 million copies worldwide. They appeared on *Top of the Pops* over twenty times, and performed on countless sell-out tours. Their images adorned all sorts of merchandise including, but not limited to, posters, calendars, videos, books, t-shirts, sweatshirts, bandannas, watches, keyrings, purses, mobile phone covers, dogtags, and dolls. The band also made hundreds of thousands endorsing products including Pepsi, Sugar Puffs and Creme Eggs.

The five members of Boyzone had each become millionaires many times over as did Louis and Reynolds. Six years after Louis had made a wild bid to break out of the tortuous cycle of life as a booking agent, he had become a very rich man.

The decision to split, however, sparked off bitter internal feuding with all involved making allegations and counter allegations against each other. Keating was openly criticised by former band members in the tabloids. He was accused of being Louis' favourite. "You know what, it's sad the way it all went and I think if people hadn't been all uppity about it and got up saying what they were saying, there would have been a future for Boyzone down the road to do something," says Keating. "It's gone far beyond that now and sadly we can't."

He says other band members may have interpreted his friendship with Louis the wrong way and this may have caused friction.

"There was times, because we talked all the time on the phone, that there might have been situations. But at the end of the day, I was kind of the channel. I spoke to the band and I spoke to Louis. Not all of the lads would call Louis every day, so I was passing everything on to Louis and likewise if the lads had a problem, they'd come to me, and I'd call Louis and say 'Louis, this is the story'."

Louis was more vehement in his response to criticism levied at him from the band members.

"It's human nature. They always forget. They always forget the good things. I don't really care because I'm in the music business forever. I'm always going to be in it and want to be in it.

"They're lucky they got the break in the first place. But you know what, I would pick them all again. That's the only thing I could tell you. I would definitely pick the five guys again for Boyzone, because they were great fun and they were great personalities."

A large number of people involved in the management team say getting rich was never Louis' main goal with Boyzone.

According to Paul Keogh, Louis "wasn't that interested in money. He didn't do Boyzone for the vision of being rich and famous. He did it, I think, because it was something he always wanted to do, and it allowed him to live the lifestyle he wanted without having to . . . " Keogh stops for a moment, before continuing. "In early days, Louis would always be the one in the queue on the guest list, half way back, and then people would say 'Oh there's Louis Walsh again' and now he's probably managing all the guest lists and that's the difference."

Louis had always been known for knowing everyone on the music scene in Dublin. Now, he knew most of the influential people in the music scene in the UK. As Boyzone had become more successful, Louis had ensured that they only dealt with the best in any given area of the business. They only worked with the best pop producers and songwriters. Their A&R person was Colin Barlow, their agent was Louis Parker, head of the huge Concorde artist booking agency, and their PR was handled by the respected Outside Organisation.

Louis had taken on the music industry at its own game. He had won, and now he was part of it. Many pop band managers only ever handle one major act, but Louis was too ambitious, and too energetic, and enjoyed the experience far too much, to sit back and savour his achievements with Boyzone. There were more acts to manage, and more No. 1s to celebrate. That said, nothing else after Boyzone would ever be quite as exciting an experience. He would never have as steep a learning curve again, never again experience the heady unbelievable thrill of guiding a group to a No. 1 hit for the first time. He would never again gaze in awe and delight at one of his acts on a magazine cover in the way he did when Mark Frith showed him the photocopied cover of Boyzone, and he knew he had made it.

Boyzone might have been finished but a new act had risen from the ashes: Ronan Keating. Louis had always maintained a closer bond with Keating than with any other members of Boyzone, and he had nurtured Keating carefully. He believed Keating and Gately were the only ones with a real chance of solo success. But he didn't believe he could manage both.

"I couldn't manage both of them," says Louis. "I probably would have, but I know Ronan definitely wouldn't have wanted that. I think I would have kicked Stephen up the arse a lot more. He needed that from someone. I don't think he was surrounded by people that were honest with him.

"He had come from a really big band, and I think he thought he was just going to automatically have fame. Ronan knew he had to work and start all over again. Stephen, he'll always be involved in the music business. He could always be working, always be on TV."

Choosing to manage Keating wasn't a difficult decision for Louis. Those in the Boyzone management team had considered Keating a great deal shrewder than his fellow entertainers.

"People have asked, 'Was that obvious at the start?'," says Keogh. "It wasn't, but it became very obvious. Shane didn't take enough time to understand the industry, Keith was the party man, Mikey never forgave Louis for not being the lead singer when he started.

"Stephen probably would have thought he would have a better chance as a solo artist, but I don't think he really spent the time to understand the business like Ronan.

"Ronan knew who was important. Ronan knew it was like 'I'll do an Elton John gig and that'll get me this'. He was well calculated in everything he did and he stuck with Louis as well."

Music journalist George Byrne agrees with this analysis. "It was obvious from very early on that Ronan was the golden boy.

Keogh acknowledges the three Boyzone members who didn't sing on the albums did not pull their musical weight to the same extent as Keating and Gately.

The three clearly would not have found it as easy to further their international careers in pop music. However, they were determined to prove Louis and others wrong. Graham had always been the odd one out in Boyzone. There were the two that could sing, the two that couldn't sing, and there was Graham.

He harboured ambitions of being a singer-songwriter but when Boyzone split none of the major labels were interested in signing him.

Undeterred, he launched his own label, Public Records, and released a single called *You're My Angel.* The single reached No. 13 in the UK.

Graham's career was more successful in Germany and Central Europe where his music was better received. No further singles were released in the UK until April 2001. The single *You Could Be My Everything* reached only No. 63 in the UK. A planned tour of the UK and Ireland was cancelled as Graham pleaded "nervous exhaustion". For the time being at least, Graham's solo career was put to bed.

Few onlookers expected Lynch to have another go at the music business. All he had ever wanted from Boyzone was to get "rich, laid and famous". When Boyzone disbanded, he spent his time racing cars on a semi-professional basis for Ford. In 2001, in an interview, he declared that his true musical love had always been hip-hop and he was forming a new act with Ben Ofoedu, formerly of Phats & Small.

The new band, a four-piece called Redhill, planned to release its first single in the summer of 2001, and then in January 2002, but no single appeared.

Lynch did have a little post-Boyzone success, in the form of a cover of Milli Vanilli's *Girl You Know It's True*, which he recorded with Duffy. The song reached No. 36 in the UK charts. It later emerged that it was recorded it as a joke. Milli Vanilli were a band best remembered for not singing on their own records.

Duffy secured work as a presenter on RTE's Pepsi Chart Show. He also hosted the childrens programme *FBI* before appearing in *Celebrity Big Brother*. The resultant hype helped his career along considerably, most recently with his appointment as *Coronation Street's* latest bad boy. He still found himself drawn to the music business, however, and has recently formed a new Irish boyband called Broken Hill, which he co-manages.

Gately never achieved international success as a solo artist. He was signed by Colin Barlow at Polydor, which released his first single *New Beginning* in July 2000. The single went to No. 3 in the UK. The follow-up singles *I Believe* (from the Billy Elliot soundtrack) and *Stay* made it to No. 11 and No. 13 respectively, and his album, also entitled *New Beginning* reached No. 9.

Despite his reasonably successful showing, Polydor dropped him. Barlow blames the media for the singer's failure to become a solo artist. He says the album was "fantastic" but it was "horrible" when the Boyzone fans did not remain loyal to Gately.

"I think he made a brilliant record. It's just that the audience, with Westlife coming along and Ronan going solo; they decided to put their money on those two and Stephen suffered from that really. And also the media were the same, because the media decided to back Ronan and didn't give Stephen the coverage he deserved and made it very difficult. *New Beginning* was a great record for Stephen and it was a shame that the media didn't give it the attention that I think it deserved."

After his attempt at becoming a solo artist, Gately took Louis' advice and sought work in musicals. In Autumn 2002, he was offered the lead role in a forthcoming production of Joseph and the Amazing Technicolour Dreamcoat in Liverpool, apparently on the recommendation of Andrew Lloyd Webber. After the Liverpool run, the show was set to go to London's West End for a six-month run.

The one member of Boyzone that Louis has continued to manage has seen his career go from strength to strength. Keating was always closest to Louis. They shared a similar taste in music and similar views on how to get ahead in the business. Even when Keating was in Boyzone, Louis ensured that he was regarded as a star in his own right.

In 1997, he co-hosted the Eurovision Song Contest and presented the Irish National Entertainment Awards, which featured the bizarre sight of him opening the envelope for *Entertainer of the Year* and pulling out his own name. In the following year, he presented the 1998 MTV Europe awards and the 1998 Miss World, and found time to be Grand Marshal of the St. Patrick's Day Parade in Dublin. He was appointed to Ireland's Millennium Committee in 1999 and was supposed to produce a celebratory song, but never did. He cited his busy schedule and media criticism as the reasons for this.

Keating released his first solo album in 2000. It succeeded with song-writing contributions from Gregg Alexander of The New Radicals, Bryan Adams, Barry Gibb of The Bee Gees, and Pat Leonard, Madonna's producer. The first single from Ronan, *Life Is A Rollercoaster*, went to No. 1 in July 2000, as did the album itself in the following month. The other two singles from the album, *The Way You Make Me Feel*, and *Lovin' Each Day*, made it to No. 6 and No. 2, respectively. In total, *Ronan* sold over 4.4 million copies.

The former members of Boyzone are now deeply divided. In a documentary entitled *Smash: The Boyzone Story* broadcast on ITV, members of the band made it clear they were unhappy about the way the band broke up.

"Myself and Stephen sang the first song," explained Graham, "which kind of really launched us in Ireland as a band and then after that I don't know how it happened at all, I really and truly don't. But for some reason Ronan just started becoming the front person. Him and Louis got on well together and obviously Louis was the manager and the next thing you know Ronan was singing everything.

"And it wasn't because nobody else could but none of us really know the reason for that one."

Although Paul Keogh was interviewed for the documentary, he says he didn't realise how bitter relations between the former Boyzone members had become. "I saw that programme, I didn't realise that they had all split in their own way. It was sad, because they were close at one stage. I think I'm no longer the enemy. I think Ronan is the enemy now. I think that the dartboard has his face on it now and not mine. I think that's funny and in a sense that's not Ronan's fault. If they had the ability they would be more successful as solo artists and wouldn't give a damn about Ronan, but it was just Ronan that had the wherewithal to keep going."

Keogh continues: "The great thing about Louis was he knew what it was. He knew it was pop music and not to take it too seriously and his great ability was to keep the guys together for as long as he did. You could see it coming, you could see that he knew Ronan was the only long-term hope he had and then the other guys saw favouritism, and it was inevitable it was going to split."

11

MUMBA ONE AND MUMBA TWO

S tar quality is a difficult thing to define. Female superstars more than anyone else are different; they glow. Their skin is luminous, their eyes sparkle and their smiles are gracious. They are toned but not muscular. They are svelte, not skinny. They are glamourous, but in a restrained and tasteful way. Above all, they have an ineffable beauty that no money can buy. Carefully applied makeup, a good haircut, some nice clothes and a personal trainer can only do so much. True stars are beautiful. Most women can only dream of being like this; can only gaze longingly at images of modern goddesses on billboards and in glossy magazines. Not Samantha Mumba; she was born to be a superstar.

Louis signed Mumba before she left St. Mary's school in Drumcondra, a leafy suburb on Dublin's northside. When she was introduced to Louis, she was already a child star. She had performed with the Billie Barry stage school since the age of three, and made her first television appearance when she was four years old. She was a beautiful and talented child but that wasn't the only reason she stood out: she was black. Her mother had been an Irish air hostess and through her work, had met and married a Zambian flight engineer.

Mumba's skin colour lent her an exoticism in Ireland and when she performed as part of an ensemble, she immediately caught the attention of the audience. She was also a natural performer with a good singing voice and a strong stage presence.

In September 1998, when she was 15, she got the lead role in a show called *The Hot Mikado*. While this performance garnered her some good reviews, it was an appearance on the RTE talent competition *Let Me Entertain You* that launched her career. The show's producer put Mumba in touch with Robbie Wootton, who had managed the Hothouse Flowers and the Black Velvet Band. Wootton also owned The Factory recording studio. He saw potential and set about grooming Mumba into a professional singer. According to Mumba, the manager showered her with gifts and spent thousands on photo shoots. However, she had not signed a management contract.

A chance introduction brought Louis into her life. Mumba's mother Barbara knew Olan McGowan, the A&R representative for Sony Ireland. Through tentative talks with McGowan, who was struck by the teenager's looks and ability, Barbara Mumba was next introduced to Dave Matthews, the US head of Sony. After the initial coming together, he passed her case to Richard Stannard and Matt Rowe, who had produced most of the Spice Girl's hits. Stannard and Rowe were eager to work with Mumba and with UK music publisher Kate Thompson, arranged to meet her in Ireland. As Mumba was performing in panto, the group could not meet to talk until late in the evening. They decided to discuss matters over drinks in Lillies Bordello, a Dublin nightclub. Wootton wasn't present that night but Louis happened to be there.

"Samantha made a bit of an entrance," recalls the singer's mother. "It was just one of those things that you actually couldn't set up if you tried. If you were trying to influence Louis, you couldn't have planned it better. Louis happened to be there and the producers introduced Samantha. A little while later, Louis came over to me and said he had actually been hearing a lot about Samantha, and had been trying to get in contact already.

"I think when he saw her that night, it sort of clicked. At that point, he just said he was very interested in managing her. But he wouldn't discuss business in a nightclub, so he'd call me the next day.

"I was like 'Yeah, OK', really not thinking anything of it, thinking 'oh, you know, nothing's going to happen.' But he called."

Louis says Mumba instantly impressed him. The company she was keeping in Lillies Bordello that night also impressed him.

"I said, 'If she's with the Spice Girls producers, she must be talented. That got me interested immediately, so I said, 'I want to manage you,' just like that. She said to me, 'But you haven't heard me sing.' I said, 'I don't care. I still want to manage you. You have it all.' I just knew there was a talent there."

He says she instantly reminded him of a young Janet Jackson or Toni Braxton. Until that moment, his international success had come with boybands but he knew Mumba was too good an opportunity to pass up.

For Mumba and her mother, Louis was too good an opportunity to pass too. He had an enviable track record and a bulging contacts book. Although his offer of management was impulsive, he had excellent credentials. Louis left the meeting that night not knowing whether he'd sold himself properly or not.

What interested him now was to find out whether he could make a deal.

Barbara Mumba, however, didn't trust anyone as far as her daughter was concerned. Her only desire was to secure the best management deal possible for her daughter; be it with Wootton or Louis. Barbara Mumba was already a survivor. She had raised her daughter and son, Omero, single-handedly. She was reluctant to move quickly in the fear of making a mistake.

"When Robbie came on board, I told him that I wanted to wait. I didn't want to just make major decisions that would affect Samantha's future. I wanted to see how things would go. I just thought, 'I don't want to sign on the dotted line with anyone just yet.' I just wanted to wait and see what happens.

"At that time, everybody was very aware of who Louis was," she says. "Louis himself didn't have a profile. There were never pictures of him in newspapers or anything. But this was my daughter and she came first. I wasn't going to just jump at any opportunity. I had to make sure it was the right thing for her and I just rang around and spoke to a few different people who knew Louis already or knew of him and it was a resounding 'Oh my God, yes, go for it'. Again, when it's your child, you can't just jump blindly into things. Although I had a good feeling personally about Louis, I obviously had to look into it."

Louis was made aware of the background checks conducted into his business and professional life. It was inconceivable that a concerned mother like Barbara Mumba would do anything else.

"The thing I liked about Barbara is that she didn't want to be one of these stage mothers," says Louis. "She just wants to be the ordinary Irish mother, living in Drumcondra. She wants her kids to be famous because they want to be famous. It's nothing to do with her. The chemistry between Samantha and Omero and Barbara together is quite incredible. It's a real unit."

Louis' credentials were confirmed by virtually everyone Barbara Mumba called. By this time, he had a professional working relationship with most people involved in the Irish music industry. Although there were those who didn't like him personally, his reputation as a manager was beyond reproach.

"When I was ringing, I was talking to people who knew both Robbie and Louis but I made the decision to go with Louis," she says. "If you're going to make a decision like that, you obviously go with the person who can do most."

Louis didn't delay in conspiring to make Mumba a star. He circulated rumours of his coup in the music industry. He wanted record labels to be screaming for her signature on a contract. Senior A&R figures in the UK quickly inferred from the noises emanating from Dublin that Louis had found something special.

In the end, Polydor secured the contract with a promise to make her a priority artist. Colin Barlow, who Louis says is the most underrated A&R man in the UK, cut the deal.

The memory of Samantha Mumba walking into his office for the first time is seared in his memory. After Louis had phoned him, knowing he would be eager to see this new talent, he had got permission to draw up a contract.

"He [Louis] said, 'Wait until you meet her. You won't believe the way she looks,' says Barlow. "She walked in my room and looked like an absolute superstar. Then I saw tapes of the talent show and heard her voice. So we actually did a deal with Samantha without any demos or anything, purely on the fact that she had a voice that was really special, and she looked a million dollars, and had a brilliant personality."

Signing a 15-year-old singer on this basis, without even a demo tape, is almost unheard of in the music industry, but both Louis and Barlow were convinced that Mumba had earning potential.

"I actually think Samantha is one of those people that comes in your office once every 10 years. She's that special and her career, if we do manage it properly, could go on to make her one of the world's biggest stars, not just in the UK," says Barlow.

Signing Mumba so quickly wasn't the only out-of-character move made by Barlow. Before the deal had even been signed, Barlow asked Mumba to go to Sweden and record some tracks with Anders Bagge, yet another one of the Swedish producer/songwriter contingent. She happily complied and, accompanied by her mother, flew to Sweden to do a little recording.

Bagge also began coaching her in songwriting techniques. Once the deal with Polydor was signed, Samantha also signed a publishing contract with Warner Chappell. According to Louis, she gets at least a 20 percent cut of the publishing royalties on every song she co-writes.

Although Samantha evidently had star potential, it was only potential. Like Westlife, she had to undergo vocal and dance coaching to bring her performances up to international pop star standards. She also worked with stylists and hairdressers to build an image that would define Samantha Mumba as a brand. She also had to learn how to promote that brand with lessons in dealing with the media. Meanwhile, work on her debut album was progressing nicely.

There were other problems though. Even though Mumba was officially signed to Polydor, she had committed herself to performing in a Dublin cabaret venue, the Red Cow Morans Hotel with the comedienne June Rodgers. Despite objections from the record company she performed as promised.

"We felt that you don't start off your career by letting someone down," says Barbara Mumba. "When she was asked to do it, she was very happy. So she went ahead and did the summer season and Omero was actually on the same show."

Meanwhile Barlow hired reputed producers including Steve Mac, who had worked with Boyzone and Westlife; Rodney Jerkins, the musical inspiration behind Destiny's Child, Jennifer Lopez and Aaliyah; and the well-known R&B team of Jimmy Jam and Terry Lewis, who produced for countless artists including Janet Jackson and Mary J Blige. The company decided Mumba should have a distinct image. Both her look and her voice dictated the style should be R'n'B-influenced, in the American style. Louis agreed with this analysis and oversaw the creation of Mumba's new image.

Her album was completed in May 2000. If she hadn't met Louis, she would have been preparing to sit her Leaving Certificate Exams. Both Mumba and her mother believed she could always go back to her studies but she would probably have only one chance of making it in the music industry.

Gotta Tell You was her first single and went straight to No. 2 in the UK charts, and reached No. 1 in Ireland, where it was the biggest-selling single of the year. Louis had another solid gold success on his hands.

Her second single, *Body II Body*, made No. 5 in the UK that October. Her album *Gotta Tell You* only went to

No. 17 in the UK charts when it was released in the same month as *Body II Body*. This was a poor showing given the success that greeted Boyzone and Westlife.

The album might not have made it to No. 1 but it did attract the attention of some big-name record label bosses in the US. Jimmy Iovine of Interscope was one. After hearing the album, he visited Dublin to meet with Mumba and Louis and signed her almost immediately. With the full backing of Interscope, Mumba had a far better shot at breaking the US than Boyzone ever had.

Iovine and Interscope had both ambition and unlimited financial resources. *Gotta Tell You* was remixed by Teddy Riley, Michael Jackson's producer, and shot to No. 1 in the US Billboard charts. While this was spectacular enough for Mumba, considering she was still just 17, it was a life-affirming moment for Louis. He had wheeled and dealed his way to getting one of his charges a US No. 1, the holy grail of modern pop music.

"It was incredible," says Louis. "It was like a dream. Her very first record . . . I'll never ever forget it.

"Iovine had worked with U2 and all that. He's probably the most powerful man in the music industry in America. He's got a great bloody team around him.

"One of his team, Brenda Romano used to call me and I used to think she was giving me bullshit about Samantha's record," says Louis impersonating an America accent, 'It's on fire. It's on here. It's on in LA. It's on Kiss and Love FM' and I just said 'Ah yeah, know the story'. But Brenda Romano made the record happen in America. She and her husband, Chris Lopez in Inter-scope, they do all the radio in America. It's the only way you break radio in America because it's such a powerful big country, 2,000 stations. MTV is important but Samantha's record went on radio and it was 'on fire' and it was massive and they loved her. It was like a dream."

Mumba's No. 1 had catapulted Louis to further heights within the music industry.

Tom Watkins, Louis' role model, greatly admired this achievement. "It's considerably different in the United States. I think he had a lot more success being Irish than I probably did, because he had that charming kind of necessary game that they wanted. Culturally, the Americans are incredibly different and they handle their music in a completely different way and you can only applaud Louis that he manipulated this No. 1."

America loved Mumba. In November 2000, *Time* commented that "Teen pop queens of late have been manufactured in a despairingly limited variety: blond and blonder, bland and blander. Samantha Mumba, 18, is a refreshing change." *USA Today* said Mumba was like a mix of Britney, Beyoncé and Macy Gray. Publicity like this helped nurture the growth of Mumba's profile in the US. Interscope used their influence to open every door they could for the young performer. They placed her as a presenter on the *2000 Billboard Awards*, and an appearance on the *2000 Radio Music Awards*, shortly after her No. 1.

Mumba's American success brought unexpected dividends. Suddenly, it wasn't just the music industry that was interested.

Hollywood took notice of this new star. Mumba was invited to do a screen test for a new adaptation of HG Wells' classic science fiction novel, *The Time Machine*, apparently after a casting agent saw her photograph in *People* magazine. She was offered the part of Mara in the film, while her little brother Omero was given the part of Kalen. By this time, further behind the scenes machinations had led to Omero being signed by Louis. The manager had convinced Polydor to sign Omero. To date, he has not succeeded in making any impact in the charts.

"Louis first saw him perform with Samantha and was impressed with him, and how he behaved on stage and so on," says Barbara Mumba, explaining how Louis came to manage her son. "After that really, it was a gradual thing. Samantha had a song with a rap on it and she fought to get Omero on the track because she didn't want another rapper on it. She knew he could do it. That then led to him doing a Disney special in the States with her, doing the NSync tour around the States last year."

Mumba is overtly supportive of her young brother. He often travels with her and she uses whatever influence she has to secure him work in the music industry.

Deciding that Mumba should go ahead and act in *The Time Machine* was easy for Louis, despite the fact that her album sales in the US were bound to suffer as she had to sacrifice months that would have been spent on touring and promotion work. "It was absolutely no problem sacrificing sales, because this film is going to be a worldwide smash. It's going to put her on the map. She even has a song on the soundtrack," explained Louis in an interview with *The Sunday Times*.

Sales were undoubtedly sacrificed for the sake of the film. Mumba's album reached only No. 79 in the Billboard album charts, and her second single, *Baby Come Over* [the On was dropped from the title for the US release] scarcely charted in the US. Another single, *Don't Need You To* [Tell Me I'm Pretty], from the soundtrack to *Legally Blonde* didn't conquer the charts either. Unfortunately, it was released on 11 September 2001.

Mumba could unquestionably have sold far more singles and copies of her album had she engaged in the intensive promotion demanded by the US music market.

"I think the album just did OK and the follow-up singles did alright, but I think she has a career there. I think Samantha's probably going to end up living in America. Probably end of next year, she'll go to America. She's definitely been offered loads of movies. I think she's definitely made for America but she'll still be successful here," says Louis. "Listen, she's only 19. She's got a big career ahead of her. It's all going to happen."

Louis sees Mumba as the next Jennifer Lopez, a star who can enjoy continued success in both movies and music.

Louis is meticulous in maximising the earning potential of his artists. Mumba was clearly someone that companies targeting the youth market could use to endorse their products. L'Oréal, for example, signed her for a major advertising campaign.

The decision to take the role in Time Machine had certainly affected her success in America. She fared slightly better in the UK, where her third single *Always Come Back to Your Love* reached No. 3 in February 2001. *Baby Come On Over* made it to No. 5 in September, and *Lately* reached No. 8 that December. She still hadn't had a No. 1 in the UK, and her album *Gotta Tell You* climbed to No. 9 but no further on its re-release in September 2001. Although her performance was respectable, it was not on a par with those of Louis' other protégés. Polydor decided not to release any further singles from the first album and sent Mumba to

Sweden to work on her second album, which was originally due out in April 2002. For undisclosed reasons, the release date of the album was delayed until 2003.

In Mumba, Louis found a completely different artist to any that had previously crossed his path. As Mumba herself has pointed out, one girl is completely different to five boys. A boyband is immediately guaranteed the support of hordes of teenage girls.

Making a star of Mumba was a huge challenge for Louis. He had the capability to turn any boyband into a profitable enterprise if he was so inclined. The only female solo act he ever managed was Linda Martin but Mumba fell into a class of her own. This has posed its own problems for Louis.

"It's easier to manage boys," says Louis. "They can work harder. They don't need any make-up artist, any stylist. They don't need all these trappings that girls need. Girls are very high-maintenance to manage. They can't take the work. They get very emotional, missing home, missing boyfriends and all that bullshit. They need stylists, makeup, hair and those people cost a bloody fortune. They're high maintenance but if they take off, they take off, and the charts are just full of girls at the moment," he says.

The crucial difference between Mumba and his other clients is that she can't be controlled as openly as Westlife.

"I'm very, very headstrong and quite independent. I think that's why Louis and myself work really well because he would be the exact same. I'm really not particularly dependent on him," she says.

"I wouldn't want him to be at all my TV appearances or interviews. I wouldn't really see Louis in the flesh that often, but I always know he's at the end of a phone line if I need him. I would hate to have a manager that was constantly with me all the time and in my face all the time and over-involved. I definitely wouldn't like that, so it works really well."

To manage Mumba successfully, Louis had to adapt his management style, both in his dealings with the artist, and with the music industry.

"Samantha is real," says Louis. "You cannot make Samantha say something she doesn't want to say. You just let her do her own thing. She's real. People buy into her because she is the girl next door."

Louis, however, makes the crucial decisions although Mumba plays this part of the business arrangement down. In reality, he makes the decisions and holds the contacts that make Mumba a star. He is also cautious about her taste in music and style preferences. He doesn't want her to become a black star in America.

"I hope she doesn't try and get too black, that's all, because she loves all that music. Being too black, you just . . . I like it mainstream, because if it's too black, it doesn't sell and I want to sell lots and lots of records," he says

Mumba likes him because he has made a point of maintaining close links to her mother, Barbara, and involving the family in any decisions he makes regarding her career.

"We have the kind of relationship where he's like an uncle or a bigger brother," says Mumba. "He's really, really over-protective of me and we'll fight like cats and dogs, but we love each other dearly at the same time. I think at times, it's a very ambiguous sort of relationship. I would look on him way more as a family friend than as a boss. I don't even think of him as my boss."

Her mother agrees. "He's become a family friend, never mind the business side of things," says Barbara Mumba. "Neither of them pull any punches. They're both very straight and they're both very loyal and those are qualities that they respect in each other. They would never hear of each other saying anything behind their back. If anything is to be said, they say it to each other's face. They're very alike in that sense. There's no pussyfooting.

"Every Christmas without fail, when Louis is en-route to Mayo to spend Christmas with his family, he always passes through our house to have a cup of tea on the way. That's become a little routine over the past few years. That's nice.

"I don't think it's like 'oh well, that's another artist and if it's not working out, I'll just replace her with someone else.' I never get that feeling from him at all.

"From my point of view, it's been a great thing with Louis from the very beginning that he has involved me so much. While initially the involvement probably was due to Samantha's age, since she turned 18, he has still continued to involve me. We discuss things regularly," she says.

In terms of packaging Mumba, Louis could not just reverse his earlier boyband strategy and market her to teenage boys. It is teenage girls who buy pop music so Mumba had to be a role model rather than a heartthrob. She comes across in interviews as articulate and intelligent, excellent qualities in a role model. That said, the definition of role model has changed over the years, hence Mumba admits that she drinks and that she sacked four consecutive stylists. She has also spoken about her sexuality.

This attitude has made Mumba seem "cool", feisty and independent but ultimately, Louis is still in control. He is far too skillful at manipulating the media to allow any of his acts to make unwarranted comments without his consent. Mumba is allowed to give her own opinions about things because she might just sell a few more records that way.

The openness only goes so far, however. Mumba's long-term Irish boyfriend was hidden away as much as possible and photographs of the couple together have rarely been published. If everyone knew Mumba had a boyfriend, the marketing machine wouldn't be able to circulate rumours of celebrity romance. She was reported to be with a slew of eligible bachelors including Eminem (who is also signed to Interscope), Craig David and Dermot O'Leary. She has repeatedly denied any such romances but the stories generated column inches when they were initially made public and so fulfilled their purpose.

Mumba, however, is similar to other Louis Walsh acts is that she is always courteous and polite with fans and journalists.

As her A&R representative Colin Barlow says, "He [Louis] is about how he expects his acts to be and I think that's good news. I think he's got good morals in what he expects from his artists. All the acts he works with, they're all really respectful and really charming people, so I think the morals that he gives his acts are really good. And if they are [badly behaved], he'll scream at them. And that's what I love about Louis, he expects high quality from people."

The biggest difference between Mumba and Louis' other acts is potential longevity. Louis knows manufactured pop acts last no longer than five or six years. The market for any individual boyband or girlband is finite. Mumba has an entire lifetime ahead of her.

"He's her manager, her protector, her mentor," says the journalist Michael Ross, who has followed Louis' career. "She will still be making records in her forties, when he is in his sixties, and if they stay together as artist and manager he will learn as much from her as she has and will from him. The next big shift in Louis' career will not be to become the manager with the greatest number of No. 1 records – he is obsessed by overtaking Brian Epstein's tally. He will eventually do that. He is too driven, too energetic and too talented not to. But if he is to be remembered as a truly great pop manager, he will have to shift to focusing on quality as much as quantity. Samantha is his route to that."

12

OPERATION AMERICA

Mumba's strike into the heart of the American music industry was part of a dual strategy involving Westlife. Although each act was signed to a different record label, Louis harboured sincere hopes for both acts in America. He was convinced Westlife could replicate Mumba's performance. He saw no reason why this feat couldn't be achieved. That the band was made up of professional entertainers reinforced this notion. By this time, Louis had developed an extremely close relationship with Westlife. In fact, the relationship was far stronger and professional than his with Boyzone. Westlife, he said, were the perfect boyband.

"You have to get five guys that get on well," says Louis. "The hardest thing with most bands is making sure they get on well. Some people are going to be more famous, more prominent, better singers and better dancers than other people."

Westlife had also shown strong endurance and stamina when it came to touring. This was a crucial part of the plan. They not only had the will to succeed, but also the commitment to take on the extra workload of promoting their albums in America. Louis couldn't risk removing Westlife from the public eye in Europe, as he had with Mumba. For that reason, he made sure the band constantly toured Britain, Europe and Asia, generating millions in concert takings.

Rather than send Westlife to America for a long single period, he arranged for them to tour Europe constantly, then fly to America for a short period, before returning home to tour once again. He wanted the band to build up a strong support base on both sides of the Atlantic simultaneously. Westlife released an unending series of records; the band worked constantly to promote their product through tours and personal appearances. Success in America would depend largely on the band's stamina. Louis saw this as no problem.

He saw the band's utter determination to make money while they were young as a good sign. It made Westlife an ideal band to take America. Louis figured that the band knew they had only a limited time. Because they knew they were disposable, he calculated that they were capable of using every ounce of energy they possessed to break the lucrative market.

"They are aware that there are other bands coming up behind them and they have only got a certain amount of years to make it," says Louis.

The band's second album though was overtly aimed at an American audience and aptly called *Coast to Coast*. Like its predecessor, it was made in collaboration with a raft of big-name producers. Louis also brought in American legends to perform with Westlife. The album saw the participation of Mariah Carey, who performed a cover version of the Phil Collins' song *Against All Odds*. The collaboration didn't perform as anticipated but the next Westlife single, *My Love*, went straight to No. 1 in the UK, breaking the record set by the Beatles for achieving successive hit records.

In the same month, *Coast to Coast* was released, amid frenzied speculation by the tabloid press, as to whether it or the Spice Girls new album would make it to No. 1. Westlife won and the album eventually sold over 2 million copies in the UK.

Incidentally, Westlife were prevented from getting eight consecutive No. 1s with *Tell Me What Makes A Man* by the actor Neil Morrissey, who released a single in the guise of children's television character Bob the Builder

Louis continued to hanker for success in America on the back of *Coast to Coast.* After the success of the group's first album in Europe and Asia, Louis sent Westlife to the US, negotiating a contract with Arista Records over there.

In April 2000, as *Fool Again* reached the No. 1 spot in the UK, Westlife embarked on a four-week tour of the US, and returned later in the year for a further six weeks. Although *Swear It Again* made No. 3 in the singles sales chart and No. 20 in the Billboard chart, which also incorporates radio airplay, the tour could not have been categorised as a success.

Arista did not release any more of the band's singles. It had been a mistake to launch the band with a ballad. American markets prefer their boybands to be more upbeat. US pop manager Lou Pearlman, for example, generally waits until the first two singles have sold well before throwing a ballad to the fans and seeing how they take it.

Westlife's failure to capture an America audience didn't deter the band. They embarked on their first major arena tour in 2001. The *Coast to Coast* tour involved 80 sold-out gigs in three continents. For this tour, they changed their performance style, using extensive choreographed dance routines for the first time. The European tour was a success.

Despite their dedication to hard labour, Westlife did not achieve any notable success in America. Although they hadn't failed completely; they hadn't succeeded either.

"It didn't matter," says Louis. "They have everywhere else in the world. They don't need America. It's going to take a chunk out of their career everywhere else, but it doesn't really matter."

When the European tour ended, RCA wasted no time in putting out another album to please and placate the fans. Once again, Steve Mac, Wayne Hector, and Cheiron had been churning out the songs, although Westlife themselves wrote five of the tracks on this album. *The World of Our Own* album was released in November 2001, and went straight to No. 1, as did the first single from the album, *Queen of My Heart*.

"They broke all the rules of all the boybands. They are much bigger than Take That or anybody else. Nobody else has ever sold the tickets they've sold. They did five Earl's Courts. U2 did four. Madonna did four," says Louis.

Although Westlife's performance in America was partly overshadowed by Mumba, it didn't matter. The band had proven itself to be a financially profitable product.

"I think I have the most honest relationship with them I've had with any band. It's honest. There are no passengers in the band at all. They have all got talent. I think Shane is the best pop singer I've ever worked with. He is the most commercial. Mark is a brilliant soul singer and it's the combination of the soul singing, and the pop singing that makes it fantastic. Kian is just like a brilliant music man all around. He's just like a rock guitar player. He plays like 12 instruments. He keeps the whole band together. And then Nicky does so much work off-stage that nobody knows about, and he's got a great look. He's a great singer. He's a great dancer. He's like the sex symbol of the band, I suppose."

Of Bryan McFadden, he says: "We didn't always get on". "I didn't like him at the start. I thought he was a loose cannon. I thought he used to drink too much, I thought he was promiscuous. But you know what, he's not. He's a really good guy and he's totally misunderstood by the media, because he looks like he's always drinking and having a good time. He did it once or twice in his life and people only know that about him. I think I will be working with him for a long time to come."

Westlife were not the only product Louis had difficulty with in the American market. Keating was signed to Interscope, which spent $300,000 on a new video for *Lovin Each Day* but it failed to deliver. The single hardly registered in the US. It went unplayed by MTV and sold only 25,000 copies. In fact, Interscope is rumoured to have spent $2 million on launching Keating in the US, but the poor performance of the single caused the record company to drop its plans to release the album *Ronan* over there.

In general, however, Keating's solo career has been a success. Thus far, he has had three No. 1 singles and two No. 1 albums in the UK. Over 6.4 million copies of his albums have been sold. Yet he still does not enjoy popularity or acclaim in his home country.

Colin Barlow is completely perplexed by this. "I think Ronan has been as, if not more, successful as a solo artist than he was in Boyzone, certainly worldwide. I find it amazing that probably the worst territory for Ronan is Ireland . . . [it's] just a crying shame that the fact he enjoys life and likes nice things people find offensive in Ireland. We've done six million albums with Ronan so far and I think that's phenomenal, and it's a shame that he'll go back to Ireland and not have the love that I think he deserves. It's a shame, because he's such a good man and he's never been an arrogant person or anything. I find it amazing the reaction he gets in Ireland. I think it's really wrong."

After his successes with boybands and a female solo artist, Louis was confident that he could conjure up a successful girlband, particularly with the help of John Reynolds, who agreed to act as co-manager. It proved a difficult venture, however, and by 2002 Louis was still trying to kickstart his girlband's career.

At auditions in the Red Box nightclub in the summer of 1999, Louis had chosen the members of his new group: two sisters, Ciara and Cathy Newell from Galway, and three other girls, Kelly Kilfeather from Sligo, Tara Lee from Dublin and Paula O'Neill from Cork. All were still in their teens. Louis called the group Chit-Chat. For a year and a half, the girls were pop stars in training. They toured with Boyzone, performed at minor concerts around Ireland and appeared regularly on RTE television.

As he had done with Boyzone and Westlife, Louis proved that he could be brutally determined in his quest to turn out the perfect pop group. Just as Chit-Chat was about to go before the cameras for its first television appearance in January 2000, Louis decided that the fivesome should become a foursome. Paula O'Neill was out because she "just didn't fit in", according to Louis. He maintained that Paula was more suited to performing as a solo singer.

Paul Conroy of Virgin signed the group shortly afterwards with a three album deal worth £1 million. The group's name was changed to Bellefire, because Virgin executives believed Chit-Chat was too reminiscent of an adult chat-line.

With the record deal signed, Louis and the Bellefire girls could concentrate on preparing songs for the group's debut album. Again, Louis found a respected pair of producer/songwriters to work with. Greg Fitzgerald and Tom Nichols had already worked with major female acts such as All Saints and Kylie Minogue. With the album ready, the band headed off in early 2001 to support Westlife on a European tour and followed this with the release of their first single, *Perfect Bliss*. The single was well received at home and made No. 2 in the Irish charts. Unfortunately, it didn't get any further than No. 18 in the UK. Virgin was happy to keep Bellefire on its roster, however, as the group had brought life to an old pop cliché by making it big in Japan. *Perfect Bliss* had shot to the top of the Japanese charts in August 2000.

Virgin decided to capitalise on this success by releasing Bellefire's album in Japan as quickly as possible. The album was called *After The Rain*. It was presented to the adoring Japanese public in October 2001 and quickly sold over 125,000 copies. A follow-up single from the album, *Buzzstyle*, was released in Japan in November and also reached No. 1.

In the same month, the Bellefire publicity machine in Ireland was cranked up with the screening of a documentary on the girls and their bid to become pop stars. *The Next Big Thing*, made by Frontier Films and shown on RTE, even generated a little controversy as Virgin sparred with the production company over the inclusion in the film of comments made by Louis. While being interviewed for the documentary, Louis said that only Kelly and Ciara were really good singers and the other two had no hope of a solo career after Bellefire. Virgin wanted the comment cut out of the programme but Frontier Films kept it in.

Bellefire's next single, a cover of the U2 classic *All I Want Is You*, was not released until March 2002 in Ireland and April 2002 in the UK. It made No. 5 in Ireland but just as the group's first single had, it went only to No. 18 in the UK. Virgin was not happy. In May, just after Paul Conroy had left the company, Bellefire were dropped. The girls discovered this news when someone showed them an article in *The Sun* about it while they were on their way to record their first performance for *Top of the Pops*. Disillusioned by the hard-edged nature of the music industry, Tara Lee left the group and was not replaced. Louis says he has "nothing at all bad to say about her". He acknowledges that she is "gorgeous looking" but says "she just didn't want it."

Although Virgin was unconvinced of Bellefire's potential, Louis remained ebullient. He was sure the trio of Cathy, Ciara and Kelly could still make it. By July, he had succeeded in negotiating a new record deal for the group.

"They're signed with Christian Tattersfield in East West Records, one of the brilliant A&R men in the UK, different than all the pop guys; signed David Gray, signed Morcheeba, works with the Corrs, works with Oxide and Neutrino. Great guy, sees them totally different to anybody else, signed them."

Louis believes that Tattersfield is the "major ace card up the sleeve" and says he is going to take Bellefire in a new direction. "The music he's sending me, it's very unusual sounds, almost American, kind of Avril Levigne type records, with a touch of the Madonna new stuff as well in it. He is a real A&R man."

The group plans to release its debut album in late 2002 but the girls have a lot of work to do to rebuild their own confidence and to convince the fans they are worth supporting. At an appearance in the free O2 in the Park concert in Dublin in August, Bellefire was roundly booed by the crowd. The group had spent most of the rest of the summer gigging on the Pop Party Tour in various Butlins camps around the UK. Bellefire's prospects may well have sunk too far to ever be resuscitated. If Louis can make a success of them now, it will be one of the greater achievements of his career. As ever, he is supremely confident. "Virgin have got them ready. They've spent the money. They've educated the girls," he says.

In 2001, Louis became a household name in Ireland, not because of his acts but because of his increasing tendency to publicly attack his critics and the vehement way he dealt with his opponents. Rarely a day passed without his name being mentioned in the press. It often seemed that it was part of a grander strategy of media manipulation.

Louis is unquestionably a driven character when it comes to his work but manipulating media coverage is not a skill that someone can acquire overnight. Louis learned how to deal with the media when he worked for Tommy Hayden Enterprises. Hayden made it clear that keeping the media on side and generating positive media coverage was one of the most critical factors in the success of an act. Louis has admitted in the past that keeping the press on side in those days often meant delivering an envelope with a £20 note inside along with a press release. This tactic is rarely used these days.

Once Louis became manager of Boyzone, he put the lessons he had learned over the years to good use. He became infamous for concocting false stories about Boyzone and other acts subsequently but remains sanguine about this.

"You give them a story and they only print it if they think it's going to be a good story or sell papers. I mean, I don't make up the stories all the time. Sometimes I do. You just give them the story or tell them something about the act."

"Everybody makes up stories," says Louis. "We're just more honest about it. The one everyone talks about and it got totally blown out of proportion was Boyzone making the video in Australia and they had a problem with the plane. I leaked it to one of the papers and it was on the news. It got totally blown out of proportion. It's nothing nobody else hasn't done. All the other bands have done it. We're just more upfront about it. I'd do it again. I'd probably tell their parents the next time in case they heard it on the news."

He is aware, however, that there is such a thing as over-exposure and is careful not to get too much publicity for his acts.

"People are going to get fed up and say 'Not that one again. I'm fed up listening to that one again.' I think Kylie is over-exposed. She's had one good record in the last few years and she's totally over-exposed."

In 2001, Louis' success in the charts and his clever propensity to generate newspaper headlines caused him to become a hate-figure for the Irish rock fraternity. The success of Westlife, Keating and Mumba provoked scorn; soon it became trendy to criticise

Louis Walsh. As his success grew, rock bands came out on the offensive and he was openly attacked.

"Louis Walsh is the worst fucking thing that has happened to Irish music in the last couple of centuries. Phil Lynott is probably fucking turning in his grave," Mark Hamilton, the bass player with the rock band Ash, said in an interview with *Hot Press*. The band had already set fire to 300 Westlife CDs while on a publicity tour for their fourth album, *Free All Angels*.

"Westlife are just the most bland band on the planet ever," commented Tim Wheeler, Ash's lead singer.

"Every single one of their songs is like a power ballad that sounds identical to the last one. It leaves you longing for some real bands, real music."

Wheeler said it was really Louis they had a problem with, as the pop manager had said Ash would not even sell 500 records. At the 2001 Ivor Novello Awards, while accepting a gong for Best Contemporary Song, Wheeler used the opportunity to launch another attack. In his acceptance speech, he said he would like to stick the award "up Louis Walsh's arse". Predictably, Louis responded in kind: "I know they[Ash] are frustrated. [Tim] is a dreadful fucking singer. He can't sing live. I said to him on the way out, 'I'll be here next year, you won't'."

Ash was not the only Irish rock band that has issues with Louis. Rory Gallagher of The Revs openly criticised Louis and the music he pushes.

Gallagher has went so far as to write an "Open Letter to the Irish Music Industry". In the letter, he slated the Irish and UK offices of the major record labels for concentrating on "manufactured" Irish pop acts rather than "genuine" Irish rock acts. These offices, according to Gallagher, "are doing a great disservice to the Irish public and to young Irish musicians. They are insulting us with their mindless regurgitated manu-factured bubblegum rubbish."

A month after the "Open Letter" was published, The Revs released a single *Alone With You*. Unusually, it was the B-side of the single that received the most press attention. It was called *Louis Walsh* (Says Rock n Roll is Dead), in which the band lampooned "karaoke" pop bands and the soulless DJs that play their music. The Revs had heard Louis announce the death of rock and roll during an interview with the Irish DJ Tom Dunne. It was an off the cuff remark but The Revs decided to make the most of it.

Louis wasn't perturbed. He didn't take the criticism from rock bands terribly seriously. He even wishes them well.

"Ash and The Revs and all these, some of these bands are very good. They work fantastically hard. They've been pretty successful. Ash have sold about a million albums and I'm not going to slag them off. They've worked really, really hard all around America and everywhere. Their singer is not the best singer in the world but they work hard and best of luck to them. It's tough enough out there," he says.

"I don't know why they slag all the pop bands. It's probably easy. Yeah, it's easy. You never see the pop bands slagging the rock bands and the pop bands work harder because it's harder to sell pop. You have to do a lot more promotion and stuff. Ash burning Westlife CDs? That was a joke! Ash are from Belfast. Westlife broke all the records ever in Belfast. Ash wouldn't sell a thousand tickets in Belfast. Deep down, I love them for the way they've worked hard. They should just get on with it."

While Louis was magnaminous towards his rock foes, fans of rock and indie music continued to develop a hatred for his methods and the music his acts perform. The vehement dislike from some elements of the public began to worry Keating and his other friends.

"I was at that O2 gig in the Phoenix Park and I saw a banner that said 'We hate Louis Walsh'," recalls Keating. "I thought I should say something when I was on stage, and then I thought 'Nah, what's the point in bringing attention to it.' At the end of the day, they don't realise that they're giving Louis press and he loves all of that."

Keating makes the point that few major rock critics or singers target his manager.

"Everyone has these great stories about Louis. I remember Bono telling me the story where U2 met Louis and said 'Listen, we don't know about this Paul McGuinness fella. What do you think?' and Louis said 'Stick with him. He'll make it happen for you.' U2 stayed with him. Louis could have turned around and said, 'Yeah I'll manage you, no worries' but he believed in Paul McGuinness and look where they are today."

13

POPSTARS

Louis had reached the pinnacle of his career by 2001. Not only those that he counts as friends, but his fans, critics and enemies began wondering if he would consider retiring. That September, he offered a clue when it was announced that he would be one of the judges on the Irish series of *Popstars*. Although he would manage the band, he said it would be his last.

Louis didn't own the Irish franchise to *Popstars*. The franchise was purchased by an Irish production company called Shinawil in early 2001.

The firm's managing director Larry Bass reckoned that he would have to involve Louis if he were to make the programme a success.

"I think trying to do a Popstars-type TV show, if you didn't have Louis in a market the size of Ireland, it might be a little bit of a damp squib, but he would transcend the market and make it interesting and worthwhile."

Louis was reluctant to get involved in the programme. He didn't want the publicity. While the public knew the name Louis Walsh, few people knew what he looked like. His anonymity would be gone forever.

"That was the biggest thing he had to get over," says Bass. "He was really laying himself up for a fall. He didn't need to do it. He had enough acts."

Several years before, Louis had been unsure of himself when he started managing Boyzone in the middle of his life, he found that the events which shaped the creation of Boyzone were the most valuable in his life. He had come close to finding genuine happiness. Nevertheless, the lessons he learned during the Boyzone years left him with a desire to face down his fears. "I was afraid to do it," says Louis, "because I've never been on TV apart from the one time I did the *Late Late Show*. To go on, and to have the cameras around, I didn't really want it and contrary to what people think, the money I got was absolutely buttons."

He did, however, believe *Popstars* would make great television and eventually agreed to take part. Within a day of his decision, he had convinced Simon Cowell of BMG to offer the Irish Popstars a record deal.

"Cowell said, 'If Louis is on board, let's do it.' That was it, end of story. I don't think you could do that with other people," says Bass.

Cowell pledged to spend €2.5 million on grooming and launching the resulting group. Louis also suggested other judges for the programme, the first of whom was his friend, Linda Martin

"When Louis first suggested Linda, he said: 'In Portlaoise, down in Naas, in Claremorris and in those parts of Ireland, they will relate to her.' And that's exactly what happened," explains Bass.

The second judge was independent television producer Bill Hughes, who made most of Boyzone's early videos. Hughes was a last-minute replacement for RTE DJ Gerry Ryan, whom the broadcaster pulled from the programme shortly before filming began.

Over 5,000 young people turned up at the Popstars auditions around the country. In Dublin alone, there were more auditionees than there had been in all the UK *Popstars* auditions put together. Martin says it was clear that most of those who auditioned had no understanding of the realities of life as a pop star.

"They had this romantic idea about showbusiness. That Louis is going to choose them, he's going to completely transform their appearance, hand them over to a record company, who are going to catapult them to No. 1 and the CDs are going to sell and they are going to become superstars. They had absolutely no realistic view about the whole process at all," says Martin.

Popstars is a franchise, which follows the same formula in every country. In the course of the 13 part series, thousands of entrants who auditioned were whittled down to 32 finalists. These were taken to a hotel in Portumna, Co. Galway to practise their singing and dancing skills for a week. They also had other important pop star lessons; playing five-a-side football and practising yoga in a darkened room. The 32 were reduced to 12 and then to six. Once the band members were picked, they were moved into a house in Co. Dublin.

The show made Louis famous. He became a household name. Any notions that he wouldn't be recognised in public evaporated. The show exerted a force over his personal life. He could no longer walk down a street without being pointed out. Strangers said hello and asked to shake his hand. He became as famous as his clients, something that he privately felt deeply uneasy with.

Popstars became far more high profile than anyone ever imagined. While the film crew was filming, one of the six contestants chosen to participate in the band was caught lying about her age. During an introductory interview, Nadine Coyle said her year of birth was 1985, making her 16 years-old and ineligible for the programme. All *Popstars* contestants had to be 18 years old. She had been the first contestant chosen for the final band.

"She sang absolutely like an angel. Now she couldn't dance to save herself but that's something that you can teach people. But you can't teach people to sing like that and she had the looks and everything else so she was the ideal candidate,"says Bass.

Her deception provided the titillation that Popstars required and catapulted the audience ratings. Louis' persona was exposed even more. It made grim but compulsive television. Coyle became famous as the popstar who never was. Footage of her lying was broadcast at inordinate length.

"All we tried to do was tell what happened," says Bass. "We did nothing more than show the chain of events as it happened. We weren't trying to demonise her or say it was right or wrong. This is what happened and that's all we did. We let the viewers make their own minds up."

Louis, however, disagrees. "I had no control over it and it was the highest rating show of the series. Over a million people watched it . . . I was just worried about her and her family because she wasn't going to go for the UK show then because she was damaged. She was still damaged from, you know, 'liar Nadine' and all that sort of thing. She did nothing that no one else wouldn't have done. It was great for the show but it wasn't great for her."

With Coyle gone, the judges decided on 20-year-old Sarah Keating from Galway as her replacement. The final line-up of the group was fixed: Kyle Anderson, 19, from Belfast; Liam McKenna, 19, from Tyrone; Emma O'Driscoll, 19, from Limerick; Andy Orr, 21, from Dublin; Sinéad Sheppard, 19, from Cork; and Keating. The band were called Six. Once he became the group's manager, Louis started putting a record deal together.

"Literally from day one," says McKenna, "there were obviously things we were really concerned about. The whole thing with Nadine. To be honest, we had to just trust him because we had no choice."

After the programme had finished filming, Louis launched Six in January 2002. He appeared very proud of his new charges; Six was already the first *Popstars* act to have signed a record deal in another country.

Louis had asked Pete Waterman to produce the group's album, although Waterman makes it sound like a favour. "I said, 'You know Louis, I don't know what *Popstars* means in Ireland. It sounds a joke to me, but you know what, if you think that much of it, I'll do it. I don't understand this *Popstars* programme and I don't understand how you break an Irish Popstars act in England.

"But you know what, it doesn't matter. If you believe in it, I'll believe in it.' And that's the way it works."

In the eight weeks between the time the group was chosen and the day it was launched, its members underwent intensive training in Ireland, the UK and Sweden. Louis had already chosen the song that would be Six's first single, a cover of the 1972 Guys and Dolls hit *There's A Whole Lot Of Lovin.*

Waterman wasn't convinced by the choice. "I never look back as fondly as Louis looks back," he explains. "He's got a fantastic memory for old songs but unfortunately, he still looks at them with the same love as when he first heard them. When we came to do the Six record, *There's A Whole Lot of Lovin*, that was Louis' idea. Now, I've done the original! I couldn't see what Louis was talking about."

Once the single was released in February, it went straight to No. 1 and eventually went six times platinum in Ireland. It was the biggest-selling debut single ever released by an Irish artist. Six were a success, for the time being at least.

Not everyone was keen on the idea of such an overtly manufactured Irish pop band. Ronan Collins, a former showband musician and an RTE DJ criticised the new group on live radio, describing the single as "a mediocre pop song from 25 years ago, that is being made even worse now". He also said it was "lacking in creativity, imagination, any kind of musicianship, and the singing is awful.

"The only ones who get any fame – and probably ultimately will get anything out of this – are Louis Walsh, Bill Hughes and Linda Martin," he said.

Louis heard the show and his blood began to boil. He telephoned RTE and was put on air. He proceeded to insult Collins from a height.

"This is a bit rich coming from a failed showband star," he said. "You've done everything and you've failed at it all, and you hated *Uptown Girl* as well, Ronan. Get a life. You're not going to make a name on our backs. Cop on, you're a failed showband star, man. You lived your whole life doing bad cover versions in Dublin nightclubs. You've never been on *Top Of The Pops*. We don't even care if you play the record or not."

By allowing his temper to get the better of him on national radio, Louis had made a mistake. He rapidly came under fire from all directions for his comments.

In an attempt to salvage the situation, Louis made a cloying apology to Collins on the *Late Late Show* a few days later. "I only did it because I care about these six people [Six]; because they've sung, they've danced, they've cried, they've laughed. I really care about them," he said.

"Ronan is a great musician, he's a great DJ, he's a great person," said Louis, adding that he was "mortified" when he listened to a tape of the argument.

Commenting eight months later on the episode, Louis says: "It was hard work and it was blood, sweat and tears for us as well as them and then for somebody to go on national radio and just dismiss it! I was like, 'Why is he doing this?' I got on and I just told him what I really thought and a lot of people didn't like it."

RTE was happy with the success of the series and the new pop group. The television station had spent over €400,000 getting the show on air, now it needed *Popstars* to perform well in the ratings.

Louis benefited from the television series. When Louis was trying to launch other acts, much of his time was spent trying to convince the media to publicise the new group or singer. Before the line-up of Six was even finalised, the target audience recognised their faces and believed they had to come to know these young people a little. An hour of prime-time television every week for 13 weeks and endless column inches devoted to the concept, the process, the entrants, the judges, the music and the intrigue was more publicity than Louis could dream of. Furthermore, he made sure that his other acts were not forgotten amid the *Popstars* mania. He mentioned them on camera and invited a number of his artists to meet the auditionees. Among those who made guest appearances on the show were Bryan

McFadden and Kian Egan from Westlife, Samantha Mumba and Ronan Keating.

There was no let-up in the publicity once the band had been launched. If anything, it went into overdrive. Six departed on an immediate promotional tour of Ireland, during which they even visited Kiltimagh where Louis' brother owns a pub and music venue. They performed up and down the country and attended "meet and greets" in countless record shops. The new stars also appeared on television as often as possible.

Louis pushed the band to the extreme. They were subjected to blanket media coverage. They were made available to the media. After one interview was finished, they were asked to do a second. Perhaps for the first time, Louis subjected one of his acts to too much press.

Linda Martin, who was appointed tour manager for Six, says Louis did everything possible to boost the group's fan base. She remembers one occasion where Louis brought the fans to meet the band.

"Our dressing rooms are fairly private places but all of a sudden, the door bursts open and it's Louis. He'd picked up a gang of fans from around the arena or in the street. Suddenly you have a dressing room full of people. In one case at the Point last year, the dressing-room was full because he had packed it with people all looking for autographs and eventually I said to one woman, 'Who are you with?' and she said 'I don't know. I don't even know who they are. He sort of pushed me in.' She just got caught up in the melee that was moving in. That's what he does and if Six would say 'What are you doing?' [he says] 'Don't you want to sell albums? I'm getting fans for you!'"

Success in Ireland had come relatively easy for Six. The big challenge for Louis and BMG was to break the act internationally. Even as *Popstars* came to an end on Irish television, it had already been sold to stations in South Africa and New Zealand, where the Six single would later go gold.

Building a fan base in foreign territories was nice but Six had to succeed in the UK for BMG to recoup its investment and for Louis to maintain his reputation.

Shinawil and RTE were initially in talks with Channel 4 but the show was ultimately purchased by ITV, which decided to show an edited version of the series during its Saturday morning children's show SM:TV, beginning on 20 April. BMG planned to release the first Six single in the UK on 5 August, just after the series ended. The single was never released, however, and there are no plans to launch Six in the UK until early 2003 at least.

"We're waiting for the right time to put it out because we can't put it out in between all the *Pop Idol* stuff because it'll just get lost," says Louis. "We should have put it out after the CD:UK show."

Cowell says he has his doubts about the group's prospects in the lucrative but cut-throat world of British pop, admitting that he was not at all happy with the final line up of Six. "I didn't agree with the people he put into the band and I told him that and we still agree to disagree at this point. The name was OK but I just wanted other people put in the band but Louis was the one picking so we disagreed on that." Though Cowell says Six still has "a chance" of making it in the UK.

Louis stirred the group to relative success in Ireland. In July the act's second single, *Let Me Be The One* also made No. 1 in the Irish charts, outselling Elvis by three to one. Six followed this No. 1 with another nation-wide tour of Ireland. In many respects, his managerial approach to Six mirrored Boyzone. He went back to basics, instructing the band to perform in small venues throughout Ireland. At least in his own mind, Louis made the decision that Six were at the most going to release records in Europe. He decided against bringing the band to America from the outset. Midway through the summer, he secured a film deal for Six. Filming is due to start in January 2003 and the film is scheduled for release around Christmas 2003.

"The people that are making it, 20th Century Fox, came to Louis wanting him to find actors from Ireland. They didn't want a band. They wanted actors who could sing and they came to Louis because he would be the best one to find them," says McKenna, who is adamant that this film will differ from other pop star vehicles.

"There's no point in the film where we play a band. We're just friends. The three boys know each other, and the three girls know each other and we all head off on holidays together. But even at the end of a film, we never become a band. So it's not *Six: The Movie*. The woman who is making it is very adamant that she doesn't want it to turn into *Six: The Movie* because it's got an American release date and everything already and we're never going to be going to America as far as the band goes."

Few onlookers really believed that Six was going to be Louis' last foray into pop, as he had promised it would be. When Louis was approached by the UK producers of Popstars and asked to be a judge on their second series, *Popstars: The Rivals*, he was too flattered to turn them down, describing it as a "big, big chance". His fee for the project was rumoured to be as high as £500,000.

"Pete Waterman put me up for the show. Colin Barlow asked me would I be interested and I was like – maybe. I wasn't pushing myself. I wasn't chasing it at all. I met Nicholas Steinberg and Duncan Gray from Granada on an afternoon in the Sanderson Hotel and I said 'Make me an offer I can't refuse financially' and they did," says Louis.

"They wouldn't give me all the gen because they were afraid I'd tell somebody about it because there's a lot of rivalry between *Popstars: The Rivals* and *Fame Academy* on BBC. They just told me that Waterman would be involved and possibly Geri Halliwell. I said 'I'll do it but I won't have any time to manage the band because I've too much on.' I don't want to be taking on too many bands or acts because I have to give them all time. There's only so many hours in the day. They told me the plot and I said 'give me 24 hours'. They faxed me a contract and I said 'absolutely. Let's do it'."

The new series had a slightly different format to the original UK *Popstars*, in order to keep the viewing public interested. This time the judges would choose two acts, a girlband and a boyband. The girlband would be signed to Polydor and managed by Louis while Waterman would manage the boyband and sign them to his own label, PWL. The series would run from September to December 2002 and climax with the two bands fighting it out for the No. 1 position in the UK singles charts. A Big Brother-style element was also incorporated into the show, whereby the public would choose the final composition of the bands by voting out some of the contestants, having watched them living together in the run-up to the finale.

As a member of the judging panel on the *Pop Idol* series, Pete Waterman had already developed a reputation as an impatient and brutally honest judge and there was no hint that he would soften his tactics for the new series. Louis, who had largely been restrained in his criticism of auditionees on Irish *Popstars*, was going to have to toughen up his act. A kindly middle-aged man doling out compliments does not make good television. He was more than capable of rising to the challenge. Eurovision winner Paul Harrington has joined Louis on judging panels in the past and says he isn't always kind to auditionees: "I have sat in with him on selection panels at auditions and he can be brutally honest. He shatters the occasional dream, but maybe he's saving them from something worse. This is a vicious business."

Louis was suitably caustic on early rounds of *Popstars: The Rivals* and UK tabloids began calling him the sobriquet "Louis the Lip", a title that made him sound like some sort of New York mafia mobster. About the worst of Louis' insults was uttered when one girl was warbling her way through *I Will Survive.* She found herself interrupted by Louis when she got to the line "Now go, walk out the door". He completed the line for her and indicated towards the exit.

Louis says he agreed to take part in the UK Popstars for the experience. "It hasn't taken up a lot of my time. It means I go to London every Saturday. Come on, who wouldn't love to do that? And be in first class hotels and you're meeting Geri Halliwell and Waterman. Honestly."

Louis insists he is not taking part in *Popstars: The Rivals* to increase his own public profile. "At the end of the day, my day job is I'm a band manager and I want to go back to that. I just want to manage my office and enjoy myself. I do not want to be a public figure. I do not want to be a celebrity like Simon Cowell at all."

14

LOUIS

L ouis Walsh has grown from being one of the most well-connected people in Irish show-business to one of the most well-connected people in global showbusiness. The wealthy circles in which he socialises are far removed from the poor rural town of Kiltimagh.

He doesn't look like a successful and powerful man. He looks like an unprepossessing man; he usually wears a simple leather jacket, a pale blue or striped shirt over a white t-shirt, and a pair of jeans or chinos turned up at the ends.

His appearance masks his true wealth. He owes several properties. The most ostentatious being a cottage on his own island, Inishdaskey, 15 acres of land in Clew Bay, five minutes off the coast of Newport, Co. Mayo. He maintains he doesn't visit the island too often. He bought the island with his brother Joseph, who lives in the US. He also owns an apartment in Co. Galway, and two others in Dublin, one on the exclusive Clyde Road in Dublin 4 and another on the even more exclusive Coliemore Road in the coastal village of Dalkey.

He is currently considering purchasing another home in London. In total, his personal property port-folio is worth about €2 million.

Louis is a shrewd investor. With John Reynolds, he owns a company called Postale, which has invested €1.14 million in a UK property consortium. This consortium has been actively trading properties since 1999, including a number of office blocks in London and a housing development in Co. Offaly. "It's nothing extravagant. It's very low key" says Louis.

He also owns Louis Walsh Management and is a director of five other limited companies including War Management (Boyzone), Rolo Management (Westlife), Give Me A Break Films, Tone Deaf Management and Brill Management.

With his manager's commission and his business investments, Louis has become a very rich man. His personal wealth is certainly in excess of €20 million. He has earned at least 20 percent of all his artist's royalties [excluding any songwriting royalties they have picked up], although his take from Boyzone was limited to 10 percent because of the early agreement with John Reynolds. Louis also enjoys other streams of income, such as his fee for participating in *Popstars* and other paid personal appearances. He has also endorsed products in television commercials, most notably the *Irish Times*.

Louis says he is unfazed by his riches. "It's not important now because I have it. Years ago it would have been all-important. I don't know how much money I have. I haven't a clue. Would you believe that? I don't know. My brother looks after all that for me, Frankie. He's the foxy one in the family. 'Every penny a prisoner' we call him. He's an accountant and he knows what to do with money and he respects money whereas I don't really respect it that much. It's not the most important thing in the world to me. My friends and my family, my life and my health are, believe it or not!"

He is not religious although he says he would like to be. "I think being brought up a strict Catholic didn't help me. I don't look on the Church like everybody else in Ireland. I'm very suspicious of the Church and power and all that."

He was never interested in becoming a priest, as his mother would have liked. In the rare moments when he is not working or listening to music, he likes to relax at home, watching television or one of his extensive collection of DVDs, or reading magazines. He says he chooses the décor in his apartments himself and enjoys buying furniture and art. He rarely settles down for long enough to read a book. He also likes to go for walks on the beach or meeting up with friends for dinner in city centre restaurants. He never cooks for himself. He drinks socially but has no interest in drugs.

"Drugs is a no-no with me totally, totally, because it fucks up people's heads and they just can't keep it together. Drugs, I'm totally against drugs, all kinds of drugs, even alcohol, which is the worst drug in the world especially for Irish people." He admits he tried marijuana and cocaine in the 1980s but hasn't touched them since. "I'm crazy enough. I don't need drugs," he laughs.

Louis has better things to spend his money on. He particularly likes spending time in the US. "I love going there. I might buy a place in Miami longterm to live. I'd like to. I'm going to Miami for Christmas. I'm going to go to South Beach, definitely. I love South Beach and I love LA. I love so many places around the world. On a good day, there's nowhere like Dalkey or I love going down to Connemara. I love the west of

Ireland, on a good day. Wouldn't want to live there full-time but it's great to visit."

His other passion is classic cars and his prized possession is a 1962 Silver Cloud III he bought in Christies of London in July 2001 for £86,350. The previous owner of the car was Elton John, who installed a top of the range sound system in it. The car is known as Miss Daisy because it appeared in Driving Miss Daisy before Elton John bought it.

"It's a beautiful, beautiful car," says Louis excitedly. "It's an absolutely amazing car. It's got red leather and all that. I don't drive it because I wouldn't drive around Dublin in a fucking Rolls Royce. I'd look like a pools winner. I'd look like some kind of plonker. So I can't drive it but I love it."

For day-to-day business, he drives an old left-hand drive red Jeep.

Music is the overarching passion in his life. His love of music goes far beyond the commercial pop with which his name is associated. In the space of a minute, he can namecheck David Bowie, Marianne Faithfull, Lee Hazlewood, Connie Francis, José Felicianos, Creed, Savage Garden, Dolores Keane and Mary Coughlan. All of his friends mention his huge music collection. "He has more records than Tower Records," says Ronan Keating.

How many CDs does he own? "About five, six thousand. Easy, easy, easy, and that's albums. Maybe a lot more. Sometimes I buy them twice if I really like them, to have them in each place. There are certain albums I would certainly buy twice. *Broken English* [Marianne Faithfull] is one of them. Lou Reed *Transformer*, David Bowie *Ziggy Stardust*, Dionne Warwick, Dusty Springfield. I always want to have two copies, just in case. I've loads of old albums. I keep all my albums. I've loads of old 12 inch disco records. I've a jukebox at home. I've a real Wurlitzer with all the original 45s in it like Brenda Lee and Patsy Cline and Roy Orbison and Gene Pitney. I think that was the golden age of music for me, the 45s."

Pop music, however, is his overriding obsession. He checks the charts religiously and always watches music shows on TV to see both how his acts are performing and how the competition is shaping up. "He loves songs, he loves music and he feels quite young and he lives his life through music. You can call Louis at three in the morning and he's still up watching MTV, reading magazines. In that respect, he lives it," says Keating.

His love of music is mentioned by almost everyone. Colin Barlow of Polydor summed it up well. "My impressions of Louis have never changed really. He's a complete and utter music lover and has the enthusiasm of an 11-year-old for what he does. I mean he's just one of those people who's not jaded by the music industry. He absolutely loves music. And I think he's one of those great people who's a fan of music and loves doing the job he does. There's so few people like that. He's not jaded, he's not cynical, and I think that's what makes him such a joy to work with. His knowledge of music is phenomenal. He's the encyclopedia of British pop music and country and western music."

He remains close to his family, particularly his mother, whom he "adores", according to his sister Evelyn. His mother in turn is "extremely proud" of her son, goes to Dublin regularly to see his acts in concert and hates reading anything negative about him. The relationship has become deeper since his father Frank died seven years ago. Maureen Walsh still lives in the family home on Chapel Street in Kiltimagh.

"There's three in Dublin, one in the States and five in Kiltimagh," explains Frank Walsh. "Are we close? Some would be closer than others, I would think, but that's just the nature of big families. Do we get together? Not that often, maybe once or twice a year we'd all get together."

Louis is closer to some of his siblings than others. His mother and siblings are his only family because he has never married and has no children. He acknowledges that he is, however, a sort of surrogate parent to his acts, all of whom have referred to him in interviews as a "father-figure".

In person, Louis is warm and talkative. He speaks rapidly and excitedly, particularly on any topics close to his heart. He occasionally gets carried away and rants on topics or people who irritate him. Then, conscious he is talking to a journalist, he says, "I'm just trying to give you good quotes." He is largely self-deprecating although given to the odd self-important comment. He is effusive in his praise of friends and those he admires and dismissive of those he doesn't particularly care for.

Friends say he is great company when he is relaxed. Both Pete Waterman and Simon Cowell say Louis is one of the funniest people they have ever met and both describe him as "a breath of fresh air".

The journalist Michael Ross says that he likes Louis "enormously". Why? Because "he's open, he's smart and he's a man of his word. Those are rare qualities. Rare in Ireland. Rare in the music business. Rare in people one comes across in journalism. If Louis says he will do something, he does it. He's not the most organised person I've met, he's not the most punctual, but he's among the most truthful and honourable."

He is largely an honest and honourable person but his catchphrase is "good scam, good scam". Paul Keogh may have had a rocky relationship with Louis at times but remembers that he was always in good humour. "That was the great thing about him. He was still always laughing. He used to come in even when he was earning a fortune and steal half the records off the record desks. He'd come in and all the new releases he'd pop in his bag and he'd be gone with about fifty records and nobody minded. They'd just say 'That's Louis'.

"He was, in the nicest way, a complete chancer. Not in a dishonest way. Everybody loved him even though they knew he was a rogue but yet he was very loyal to them. They didn't stick by him for any monetary gain, because they stuck by him when he hadn't a penny. Everybody's very loyal to Louis. He rings me the odd time here now, and he always says, 'Can you put me through to God please' and he still keeps the same sense of humour."

Loyal is a word often used to describe Louis by those who know him. Once a friend or an act has won his trust, it is rarely withdrawn. "Louis either trusts you totally or he doesn't trust you. There's no in-between. And I think that's the nature of that business because there are so many people knifing you in the back and it's real bitchy and all that, from what I can see. He either trusts you or he doesn't you and if he trusts you, you've got carte blanche to do anything," says his brother Frank.

His friends say his personality hasn't changed over the course of his career, other than becoming more self-confident in recent years. Louis himself agrees: "I don't think I've changed at all. I still go to Luigi's chipper in Ranelagh for my chips. I queue up with everyone else.

Why shouldn't I? I don't think I've changed. Maybe a little bit more outspoken."

In truth, no one can undergo the transition from being an ordinary nobody to a wealthy and successful person without changing in some respects. The friends he made in 1970 are still his friends today.

Carol Hanna, is perhaps one of Louis' closest and longest-standing friends. "People might think 'Oh God, that guy'. He's maybe a bit arrogant but Louis was always like that and can be very abrupt at times. I haven't seen him change as such. He was always like that, but people didn't know him then. I'd hear him talking to the ballroom owners and that years ago and he did have that sharpness. But other people probably didn't see that. It has just come out now much more so because people see," she says.

Virtually everyone who knows him personally or professionally says he maintains an almost religious devotion to professionalism.

Something Pete Waterman said while chatting about Louis gives weight to this . "Louis is . . . Louis is . . . Louis is . . . I'll tell you what Louis is, he's in total control of Louis, which means that he does what he wants to do. If Louis doesn't call me, it's not because he's forgot, it's because Louis doesn't think he should speak to me at that particular point in time. That's the way he is. Like all managers, he doesn't like confrontation. That's a part of a manager's job, to know when to confront and when not to. I would say he is absolutely superb at that."

Louis has opted to run his business himself for the most part, with only one personal assistant in his Dublin office. Those who know him are divided on whether or not maintaining the one-man-band operation is a good idea.

"What has happened Louis," says Paul Keogh, "is the same thing that has happened others; how to handle the fame of it and how to manage the influence. If I had one criticism, he's tried for too long to manage off a mobile phone and it has been to his detriment. He had all these acts, and everybody had his mobile number.'"

Other observers believe this is the key to his success. The editor of *Heat*, Mark Frith, thinks Louis' way of doing things is admirable, even if it's not the norm for pop managers. "If you had the energy to do that, then do it. Not many people do, and he certainly has energy in spades and good for him. He's got very strong people around him, like press officers, so he does have an extended family around him, a wider team around him. That's the way he chooses to be and he's a networker and he's very good at it. The only thing that would ever stop you working like that is if it got too much as it does for most people."

The fact that Louis never moved his business operation to London is also notable. Jim Aiken feels particularly strongly about this. "The place for him to have based his pop music empire was to get to London as quickly as possible, maybe get to LA as quickly as possible. Just as U2 became the dominant rock band in the business from a Dublin base, Louis was able to do the same with pop. Is that of benefit to the country? I think it's of huge benefit that we do have our own pop stars walking around. He helped to develop their careers, and more than anything else, he sold them. He's kept Dublin vibrant. He's kept us working over the last lot of years. He definitely has given more than he's got."

Journalist Michael Ross agrees: "He gave it [the Irish music industry] a sense of optimism at a time when it had none. He more or less singlehandedly raised it from the dead. The boyband phenomenon is not to everybody's taste, and certainly is not to mine, but if you look at the moribund state of the Irish music business in the mid-1990s, and look at it now, one can only conclude that Louis' success has only done the business good."

Louis loves living in Ireland. He says he couldn't manage living anywhere else. "I like here. I like the people here. I like living in Ireland. I like the pace. I like the thing that you can go anywhere you want and do anything you want to do. People just leave you alone. I like Ireland with all its faults and all its begrudgery. It's still the best place in the world. It could be a fantastic place but it's a good place.

"I do wish there was more help for starting new acts. I think we could all work so much better if there was more help here from the government, from radio, from television and from the press.

"The begrudgery thing is definitely here. People love you when you're struggling but when you make it, they think 'Ah, who does he think he is?' You do get that all the time with different Irish people. But still, I wouldn't want to live anywhere else. I pay full tax. I pay an awful lot of tax by living here. My brother Frank thinks I'm crazy but I like here. It's still the valley of the creaking windows but I like it."

Asked who he admires in modern Ireland, Louis has little trouble in reeling off a list of names. "I would definitely say Gay Byrne, Eamonn Dunphy, Sinéad O'Connor, [super-market magnate] Margaret Heffernan, [fashion designer] Louise Kennedy, Paul McGuinness, Roy Keane, Michael O'Leary, U2, Van Morrison and Enya. And obviously there're a few other people.

There's a friend of mine, Desmond Morris. I have to mention him because he's one of the people I admire most and he influences me a lot. He's one of my best friends and he's involved in one of my companies. And I suppose my mother."

Who is the real Louis Walsh? More than anything, he is someone who loves music and who is driven by that passion. He might not be a talented businessman in the accepted sense, but he is determined, he works extremely hard and is extraordinarily talented at his job. He is highly intelligent, a shrewd thinker and can be coldly calculating if needs be. He knows how to deal with people and what attitude to adopt when confronted with different types of characters. With some people, he is charming. With others, he is demanding. With others again, he is simply ruthless. He can be impetuous and impatient. He can be poor at accepting responsibility and admitting his mistakes. He is adept at generating publicity and has developed a public persona to suit his own ends.

All of this aside, he is largely a likeable and engaging person. He has many long-standing friends both inside and outside the music business and most describe him as good-humoured, generous and gregarious, a social animal who enjoys nothing more than telling outrageous stories.

Louis' most notable achievement has been consistent success in a notoriously fickle industry. Most pop managers have one hugely successful act. It's rare for a manager to maintain an entire stable of stars. Louis' client list includes Ronan Keating, Westlife, Samantha Mumba, Omero Mumba, Bellefire and Six. He recently signed Lulu.

Like him or loathe him, few deny that he has developed extremely successful products, has contributed to the Irish economy and has gained respect internationally.

"Is Louis Walsh respected by the UK music industry?" asks Frith, his friend.

"Absolutely. I don't think respect is as important as record sales and it never should be if you're a manager of a pop band. But he has respect in the sense that he could ring any MD of any record company now, and get a meeting, and they would be falling over themselves. I think that's the ultimate sign of respect. He could ring any one of the six majors now, say, 'I want to meet you three o'clock tomorrow morning, can't meet you any other time.' They would be there. They would run a thousand miles to make that meeting."

The music industry is cut-throat and competitive. It is also more fragmented, meaning there are more record companies competing for the teenage market.

Because Louis has reached the top of the business and stayed there for so long, many believe it is only a matter of time before he retires.

Tom Watkins has told Louis that the good times cannot last forever. "What I always warned Louis of was the temporary nature, the transitory nature of the whole business," says Watkins, "and how you can do your very best for all these guys in the band and in the end, they're just going to end up kicking you in the teeth anyway. So you've got to be prepared to take a real hiding at the end of it. And it will end, sooner or later."

Louis himself says he has no plans to retire from the music industry. "What would make me stop is if I got into bad health. If I thought I only had ten years left,

I'd say 'fuck this, I'm going to enjoy myself. I'm going to buy a nice apartment in Miami' but I'd probably get bored."

While he enjoys the trappings of power and success, Louis is under no illusions about the nature of his achievements.

"I don't think I'll be remembered at all. I really don't. Disposable pop music. When it's gone, it's gone. People don't buy records because . . . I always think the star is the person on the stage, not the person in the back room. The public doesn't care. It's the person on the stage that's the star, not the promoter, the manager, the producer or the A&R men.

"I think we're all lucky fuckers. I always say that: 'What are we? We're lucky fuckers'. We always say that in our business, Ronan, Westlife, all that. We're not overly talented. We're just lucky. Right time, right place.

"I'm insecure in my own little way too because I don't want this to go away. I love the high, the vibe, getting a hit record, I love it. I'm hoping to have three, four No. 1s this year and I think I'll get them. It's not the most important thing but it's fun. It's what everybody wants, to be No. 1. I'm not going to slash my wrists or anything if it doesn't happen, or cry or anything like that. I just get on with it and I never look back on the past. I always look to the future because there's no point in living in the past. It's forgotten. It's gone. It's over."

BIBLIOGRAPHY

BOOKS

Coughlan, John ed.
The Swingin' Sixties Book, (1990)
Carrick Communications

Crowley, Kennedy
A report on the Irish popular music industry, (1994)
KPMG Stokes

Fallon, BP
Boyzone: By Request,(1999)
Boxtree

Keating, Ronan and Rowley, Eddie
Life is a Rollercoaster, (2001)
Ebury Press

Pattenden, Siân
How To Make It In The Music Business, (2000)
Virgin Publishing

Power, Vincent
Send 'em Home Sweatin': The Showband Story (1990)
Mercier Press

Rowley, Eddie
Westlife On Tour, (2002)
Ebury Press

Rowley, Eddie
Boyzone: Our World, (1998)
Ebury Press

Stephenson, Pamela
Billy, (2001)
Harper Collins Entertainment

NEWSPAPERS AND MAGAZINES

Adams, Jo 'Play it again, Sam',
  The Observer, 2 September 2001

anon, 'Louis the Lip is new TV ogre',
  The Star, 4 September 2002

anon, 'Virgin in blazing row over TV show on girl band Bellefire',
  Irish Independent, 6 November 2001

anon, 'Star gazing',
  Hot Press, 14 January 2002,

anon 'Eurosong girl ill on eve of contest',
  Irish Independent, 19 April 1980

anon, 'Dreaming of a trite Christmas',
  Independent, 21 December 2001

anon 'Result means red faces at Castlebar,'
  Irish Press, 21 April 1980

anon 'Two sales-a-second for Johnny Logan',
  Irish Independent, 25 April 1980

anon 'What's another manager',
  Hot Press, Vol 3 No 24, May 23 - June 6 1980

anon 'Westlife admit defeat',
  Hot Press, 19 July 2001

Armstrong, Stephen 'When will I be famous?',
  Sunday Times, 14 July 2002

Battersby, Eileen 'Peter Pan of pop',
  Irish Times, 1 July 1999

Boland, Rosita 'Looking for six of the best',
  Irish Times, 19 January 2002

Boland, John 'Who needs facts anyway,'
  Irish Independent, 9 February 2002

Bright, Spencer 'If tomorrow never comes',
  Ireland on Sunday, 28 July 2002

Brophy, Eanna 'What's another win!',
  Sunday Press, 20 April 1980

Carey, Brian 'Brogan makes right London connection',
  Sunday Tribune, 21 October 2001

Chu, Jeff 'Go West, Young Men',
  Time, 7 May 2001

Clayton-Lea, Tony 'Mumba One',
  Irish Times, 27 May 2000

Clayton-Lea, Tony 'A star is born',
  Irish Times, 24 February 2001

Clifford, Michael 'Grist to the mill of pop's Sun King',
  Sunday Tribune, 20 January 2002

Coffey, Edel 'The girl in the machine',
  Sunday Tribune, 26 May 2002

Cooke, Rachel 'No fear, plenty of loathing',
  The Observer, 16 December 2001

Courtney, Kevin 'Critics loathe it, millions love it,'
  Irish Times, 12 May 2001

Crimmins, Carmel 'When Irish eyes are smiling, singing and
    dancing',
  Reuters, 2 May 2002

Curran, Ken and Purcell, Bernard 'A star is born (again)',
  Irish Independent, 11 May 1987

East, Louise 'A star who',
    Irish Times, 14 March 1998

Ebert, Roger 'The Time Machine',
    Chicago Sun-Times, 8 March 2002

Fay, Liam 'Boy of the Rovers',
    Sunday Times, 21 July 2002

Fay, Liam 'Six, lies and videotape',
    Sunday Times (Irish edition), 27 January, 2002

Gibson, Owen 'Children of the revolution',
    The Guardian, 22 October 2001

Gibbons, PJ 'Pop goes another band',
    Irish Examiner, 18 January 2002

Graham, Bill 'Logan's Law',
    Hot Press, vol 4 no 1 June 6 - June 20 1980

Hanafin, Will 'The bushwhacking of Ronan',
    Independent, 23 July 2002

Hattenstone, Simon 'Go on, take a pop',
    The Guardian, 21 January 2002

Haughey, Nuala 'Westlife take Christmas number one',
    Irish Times, 20 December 1999

Heaney, Mick 'Wish Upon A Star',
    Sunday Times, 30 December 2001

Humphreys, Joe 'Westlife break record with 5th number 1',
    Irish Times, 3 April 2000

Jackson, Joe 'Telling it like it is',
    Hot Press, 12 October 2000

Jackson, Joe 'The boyz in the bubble',
  Hot Press, 14 December 1994

Jackson, Joe 'Louis Louis',
  Hot Press, 16 April 1997

Jelbert, Steve 'Svengali? Me? I'm more like a butler',
  The Independent, 20 March 2001

Layne, Anni 'The Backstreet Boys and 'N Sync have company',
  Rolling Stone, 13 November 13 1998

MacMillan, Fraser 'Now he tastes the fruits of fame -
  autographs in the street, a Bentley on the doorstep',
  Sunday Independent, 27 April 1980

Meagher, John 'I'd love to come home to this country like U2
  do . . . and people shake your hand and say 'fair play to
  you'',
  Irish Independent, 6 October, 2001

Michael, Neil 'So you want to be a pop star? Meet the man
  who turns dreams into reality',
  Daily Express, 23 January 2000

Mitchell, Elvis 'In Futuristic New York Are Pods Rent-
  Controlled?',
  The New York Times, 8 March 2002

Moloney, Eugene 'Prince of pop just wants to be left alone,'
  Irish Independent, 2 February 2002

Morrissey, James 'Johnny in Hague triumph',
  Sunday Independent, 20 April 1980

Mulcahy, Orna 'Johnny come lately',
  Sunday Independent, 10 May 1987

Mulligan, Gerry 'What's another tear on the way to the bank",
  Irish Independent, 21 April 1980

Murphy, Peter 'Man and Boy',
  Hot Press, 22 April 2000

O'Hare, Colm 'We're just five culchies coming into Dublin's
  pop scene',
  Hot Press, 24 June 1998

Ojomu, Akin 'Stars in his eyes',
  The Observer, 21 January 2001

O'Toole, Bernie 'Star search offers glittering prize as RTE adds
  twist to Eurovision',
  5 August 2002

O'Toole, Fintan 'The Garda and the new gentry',
  Irish Times, 8 January 2002

Palta, Lisa and Wick, Ali 'Sir Elton's Garden Party,'
  OK, 10 July 2002

Petridis, Alexis 'The power behind pop',
  The Guardian, 23 November 2001

Porcelli, Kim 'This Is Pop',
  Hot Press, 22 June 2000

Power, Ed 'the boys are back in town',
  Irish Independent, 19 June 2002

Purcell, Bernard and Rea, Stephen 'Johnny's another year,
  another win',
  Sunday Independent, 10 May 1987

Quinn, Helen 'Loganmania as a star is reborn',
  Irish Press, 11 May 1987

Rowley, Eddie 'The Rise Of Kiltimagh Kid Who Became King
  Of Showbiz',
  Sunday World, 30 April 2000

Rowley, Eddie 'How His Big Boy Band Gamble Paid Off',
  Sunday World, 7 May 2000

Sullivan, Caroline 'A boy's own story',
  The Guardian, 4 December 1999

Sullivan, Caroline 'Battle of the blands',
  The Guardian, 13 November 2000

Swift, Jacqui 'She has no talent, can't sing or dance and like the
  kids who audition, just wants fame',
  The Sun, 6 August 2002

Walshe, John 'Angels With Dirty Faces',
  Hot Press, 12 April 2001

Walsh, Louis 'The perfect boy band',
  The Observer, 29 April 2001

Waters, John 'The Westlife era has no right to sneer at Big
  Tom',
  Irish Times, March 7 2000

Wren, Maev Ann 'Johnny comes marching home',
  Irish Times, 22 April 1980